MAGIC OF ALKALINE

Unlock the Forbidden Secrets of Ancient Power

Beneath the shifting sands of time, in the shadows of history's greatest mysteries, lies a truth too powerful to ignore

By

Daniel Di-Maio

Dedication

To my beautiful, wise, and brilliant wife, Amber—my best friend, my partner, and the light that inspires me every day.

To my grandfather-in-law, Bill Nelson, who welcomed me as family from the very beginning. Bill always believed in me—sometimes more than I believed in myself. His faith in my future, and his certainty that I was destined for greatness, remain a gift I carry with me. Thank you, Bill.

Acknowledgement

I would like to acknowledge my Uncle Charley Mayo, who inspired me to think for myself and to never stop asking questions.

To my coach and mentor, Gord Hubbard—thank you for setting me on this path and for your constant guidance and encouragement.

And to all the friends, teachers, and fellow seekers who continue to inspire this journey—I am deeply grateful.

About the Author

Daniel Di-Maio has always been a seeker of truth—unafraid to ask questions, challenge assumptions, and think for himself. A lifelong student of scripture, he is passionate about reading and studying the Bible directly, without filters, and finding meaning that goes beyond tradition.

Known for his courage to ask the hard questions—even those that may be uncomfortable—Daniel believes that true growth comes from questioning the narrative and pursuing deeper understanding.

He holds three college degrees: an Associate of Arts in Criminal Justice, a Bachelor's in Human Services, and a Bachelor of Science in Business Management. This diverse background reflects his commitment to both service and leadership, shaping the unique perspective he brings to Magic of Alkaline.

Note for Readers

Are these merely ancient relics… or gateways to an untapped energy that has been hidden from humanity for millennia?

Dare to venture deeper?

Dare to explore the unknown?

Beneath the dance of the Aurora Borealis, where charged particles meet Earth's magnetic embrace, energy is reborn, an eternal cycle, represented by the ancient Ouroboros, the serpent devouring its own tail.

The Magic of Alkaline is more than just water; it is an awakening.

Disclaimer:

The information provided on this landing page is intended for educational and entertainment purposes only. Every effort has been made to ensure the accuracy, reliability, and completeness of the content at the time of publication. However, no guarantees or warranties—express or implied—are made.

The author is not a licensed medical, legal, or financial professional. The content herein is not intended as advice in any of those fields. Always consult a licensed professional before acting on any information found on this site.

By viewing or using this site, you agree that the author and publisher are not liable for any damages, losses, or consequences—direct or indirect—that may arise from the use or misuse of any content herein, including but not limited to errors or omissions.

Affiliation Notice:

Magic of Alkaline is an independent platform operated by Daniel Di-Maio, an official Independent Distributor. This site may reference or link to Daniel Di-Maio's official business websites, which are also operated independently.

Table of Contents

The Great Pyramids _____ 1

The Ark of the Covenant_____ 2

The Great Pyramid Water of Life Connection _____ 5

The Ark Of The Covenant, Great Pyramid of Giza Connection_____ 11

The Nicola Tesla Electric Oscillator Egyptian Ankh Connection _____ 15

The Staff of Moses Water of Life Connection _____ 21

The Caduceus Water of Life Connection _____ 24

Was Yahweh a Dragon? _____ 28

Before the Flood — A Different Earth, A Different Water _____ 33

Magic of Alkaline — In the Time of the Titans _____ 37

In The Age of The Titans _____ 42

The World Before The Flood _____ 49

The Flood _____ 52

How Did They Build These Structures… Without Power Tools, Cranes, or Trucks? _____ 59

The Secret They Don't Want You to Know _____ 62

SACRED SECRETION & THE WATER OF LIFE _____ 66

The Hidden Science Behind the "Living Water" of Scripture _____ 72

Magic of Alkaline: Monoatomic Gold _____ 75

The Science of Alkaline: Where Magic Meets Molecules _____ 82

DANGERS OF TAP WATER — What You're Not Being Told_____ 85

Is Bottled Water Slowly Poisoning You? _____ 87

Professional Supper Models: _____ 97

What is the Magic of Alkaline? _____ 101

Ionized Water: The Healing Water of Life _____ 104

Fight Obesity, Save Your Life – With Ionized Alkaline Water _____ 108

Soul Shine / Unlock the Glow Within _____ 112

The Water of Life - Ionized Alkalized pH 9.5 _____ 116

Danger- Beware of Poisonous Waters _____ 120

Give Your Pets the Water of Life _____ 123

("Killing Cancer — Not People") _____ 127

Elevate Your Restaurant & Bar – The Ultimate Water Solution _____ 131

Sing Stronger, Live Better with Alkaline Water _____ 136

The 100% Green Miracle: No More Cleaners—Ever! _____ 139

Lucrative Business Opportunity: _____ 143

Tax Write-Offs _____ 146

Capital One Financing _____ 147

New Rich Syndicate _____ 149

Advertise With Traffic Authority _____ 152

The Unseen Laws of Wealth_____ 155

Can You Truly Manifest Financial Abundance? _____ 157

The Great Pyramids

Power stations of an ancient civilization?

For centuries, we have been told that the pyramids were mere tombs, but what if that was a deception?

Some researchers believe the Great Pyramid of Giza was an energy generator, harnessing frequencies and water to create an electromagnetic force unlike anything seen before.

Could this lost technology hold the key to life-altering hydration and power?

What ancient civilizations knew about water and energy may change everything we believe about modern science.

Some say the pyramid's inner chambers once surged with ionized energy, similar to the structured water technology found in Modern Water Ionizers.

Was it an ancient water purification system designed to sustain an advanced race… or something far more dangerous?

The Ark of the Covenant

A divine conduit of power?

Hidden, feared, and whispered about for thousands of years, the Ark of the Covenant was said to contain the very essence of divinity.

Ancient texts describe deadly bursts of energy emanating from the Ark, causing armies to crumble and civilizations to fear its presence.

Could the Ark have been a high-voltage capacitor, capable of storing and discharging energy beyond our understanding?

Did the water rituals of the High Priests serve to activate its hidden potential?

What if the secret of 'Living Water'—mentioned in countless sacred texts—was directly tied to the Ark's legendary power?

Some say those who understood its workings controlled life itself.

What if that knowledge was never truly lost?

The Egyptian Ankh — Water As The Key To Life?

The Egyptian ankh, often called the "key of life," symbolizes vitality, immortality, and the divine flow of energy.

Some theories suggest that the ankh represents an ancient understanding of energy transmission, similar to modern electrical circuits.

Nikola Tesla's electric oscillator, a high-frequency resonance device, was designed to generate and control electrical currents, mirroring the concept of energy flow and balance—ideas also metaphorically linked to the ankh.

Tesla's work on resonance and structured energy fields connects to the modern study of water structuring technologies.

Modern water ionizer systems use electrolysis to restructure water, enhancing its antioxidant and hydration properties.

This process resonates with Tesla's ideas on energy harmonization and structured frequencies, potentially aligning with the symbolic meaning of the ankh—life force energy flowing in a purified and revitalizing manner.

The Staff of Moses: A Tool of Miracles or Ancient Technology?

A simple wooden staff... or a device capable of parting seas, summoning divine fire, and channeling the forces of the universe?

According to the Bible, Moses struck a rock and caused water to flow—providing sustenance for thousands.

But what if this was no mere miracle?

What if the staff were a conductor of natural energy, tapping into Earth's resonance to alter reality itself?

Could the staff have been an early form of water ionization, charging and altering water to sustain life?

Was it connected to the lost wisdom of ancient civilizations that understood how energy flowed through water?

Could the same principles still be harnessed today?

The Caduceus: The Hidden Code of Life Force Energy?

The symbol of the Caduceus, often mistaken for a simple medical emblem, is far more than just a symbol.

Twin serpents intertwined around a central staff. Does this represent DNA, energy flow, or an ancient key to unlocking health and vitality?

Many believe the Caduceus represents the Kundalini force, a powerful energy that flows through the body, similar to how structured, ionized water energizes every cell it touches.

Could this symbol be hiding the truth about how energy moves through water, the body, and the universe?

Did the ancients understand how to charge water with frequencies to enhance longevity and consciousness?

Is modern water ionizer technology the modern rebirth of this lost science?

Dare to Explore… If You Are Ready

For centuries, the powerful elite have kept these secrets locked away.

What if water—charged, structured, and alive—was the missing link between these ancient artifacts and human potential?

What if the ancients understood something that we are only beginning to rediscover?

The time has come to awaken the lost knowledge and step beyond the veil of deception.

The truth is waiting for those who dare to seek it.

Are you ready to unlock the Magic of Alkaline and harness the hidden forces of the universe?

Drink wisely. Explore fearlessly. The path to ancient power begins here.

Enter the mystery — Explore the Magic of Alkaline at your own risk.

The Great Pyramid Water of Life Connection

What is the Magic of Alkaline, the connection to the Great Pyramid of Giza, and what is the science behind Ionized Water — The Water of Life?

Unlocking the Secrets of Ancient Water

For centuries, the great pyramids of Egypt have stood as enigmatic symbols of power, wisdom, and advanced technology.

But what if their greatest secret wasn't in their towering structures, but beneath them?

Beneath these colossal monuments lie vast underwater aquifers, some producing life-enhancing, alkaline-rich water, while others yield acidic or even toxic water.

Did Ancient Egypt Harness Electrolysis?

In a ground-shaking revelation, archaeologists may have uncovered eight spiral wells beneath the Middle Pyramid descending a staggering 640 meters into the Earth.

That's 4.5 times the height of the Great Pyramid plunging into hidden aquifers, where two mysterious megastructures—262 x 262m and 80 x 80m cubes—were possibly found with advanced Lydar Equipment.

And it doesn't stop there…

Inside the Great Pyramid, five new King's Chambers have possibly been discovered, aligned in the same sacred pattern as the towers of Angkor Wat, suggesting a forgotten global knowledge, an ancient energy network… and possibly the secret to longevity.

The Ancient Egyptians Knew

Hieroglyphics inside the Temple of Edfu, Abydos, and even on the pyramid walls themselves repeatedly mention:

"mw n ankh" — Water of Life

"mw nmtwt" — Poisonous Water

They differentiated between life-giving, healing water… and dangerous, acidic death-water.

Were The Pyramids Water Ionizers?

Researchers, like Dr. Carmen Boulter (University of Calgary, "The Pyramid Code") and Dr. Semir Osmanagić, have hypothesized for years that the pyramid's architecture—particularly the granite-lined King's Chamber, copper resonant elements, and north-south vent shafts—acted as electromagnetic energy collectors.

These elements may have ionized the water flowing beneath the pyramid through vibrational frequency and piezoelectric compression.

In short, the elites of the time may have had access to naturally ionized alkaline water.

Why?

Because they understood energy.

They understood healing.

And they guarded this knowledge with their lives.

While social media explodes with this brand new discovery, the truth of these new findings remains under debate, one fact stands unshaken: there are vast, ancient aquifers flowing beneath the pyramids.

Could the Pharaohs have used water to generate life-extending energy?

Was this ancient electrolysis, a natural, sustainable technology that was long buried in time?

This is NO Coincidence.

Like the possible eight newly discovered wells underneath the Great Pyramid, Modern Water Ionizers can produce similar ionized water.

Coincidence?

Modern Water Ionizers taps into the same principle: ionized, structured water created through cutting-edge electrolysis, supporting your body's natural energy, detox, and longevity, just as the ancients may have once done.

The ancients left us clues. Current Technology makes it portable.

Could this be evidence of ancient electrolysis?

A hidden technology that the Pharaohs themselves harnessed for longevity, vitality, and perhaps even superhuman abilities?

Water Fit for Kings, Powered by Modern Science

Modern state-of-the-art Water Ionizers are more than just a water ionizer; they're a gateway to the past, a modern rediscovery of what the ancients may have known all along.

Like the pyramids' hidden aquifers, modern ionization system produces a spectrum of water types, from deeply alkaline, antioxidant-rich drinking water to acidic water with cleansing properties.

Imagine having access to the same kind of water that may have sustained Egypt's elite, strengthening their bodies and sharpening their minds.

Ionized Alkaline pH 9.5 water has been linked to enhanced hydration, detoxification, and cellular rejuvenation benefits that might explain why the Pharaohs seemed to transcend ordinary human limitations.

The Hidden Science of Electrolysis & the Pharaohs' Secret

Just as the pyramids' underground wells may have naturally undergone electrolysis, separating water into beneficial alkaline and acidic properties, so too do Modern Water Ionizers.

This cutting-edge technology infuses water with molecular hydrogen, neutralizing free radicals and restoring balance to the body.

Could the Pharaohs have tapped into this knowledge to elevate themselves above the masses?

While the common people may have been left with acidic, disease-ridden water, Egypt's rulers may have reserved the most potent, life-sustaining water for themselves, just as today, you can choose to nourish yourself with the highest-quality alkaline water available.

Reclaim the Power of the Ancients

By bringing Ionized Water pH 9.5 into your home, you're not just investing in purified, ionized water—you're tapping into an age-old mystery, unlocking the potential that history's greatest civilizations may have once embraced.

Hydrate like the Pharaohs did and take advantage of Ionized Water, or better known as the Water of Life!

Energize like an elite. Experience The Water of Life, where ancient wisdom meets modern innovation

.

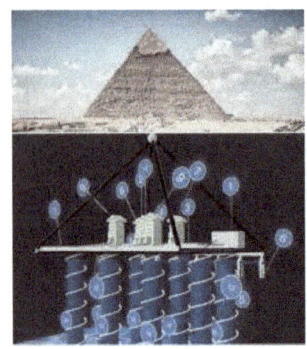  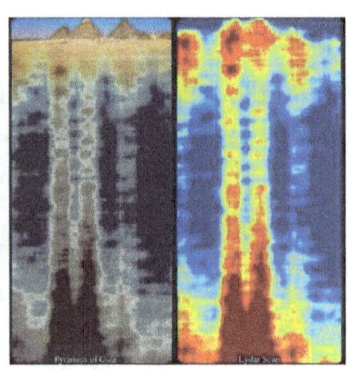

Constellation Orion's Belt

The Great Pyramid of Giza

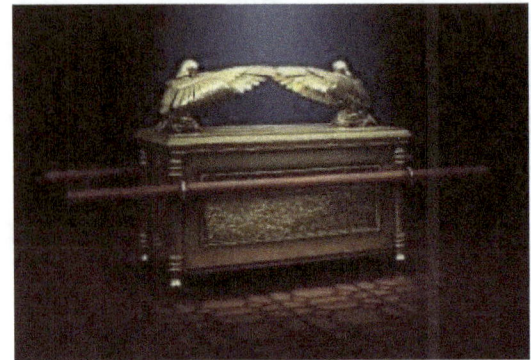

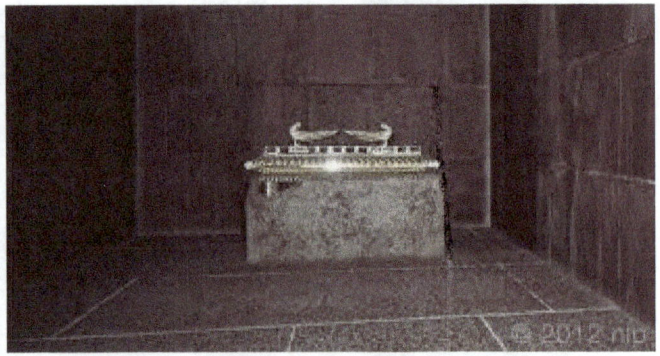

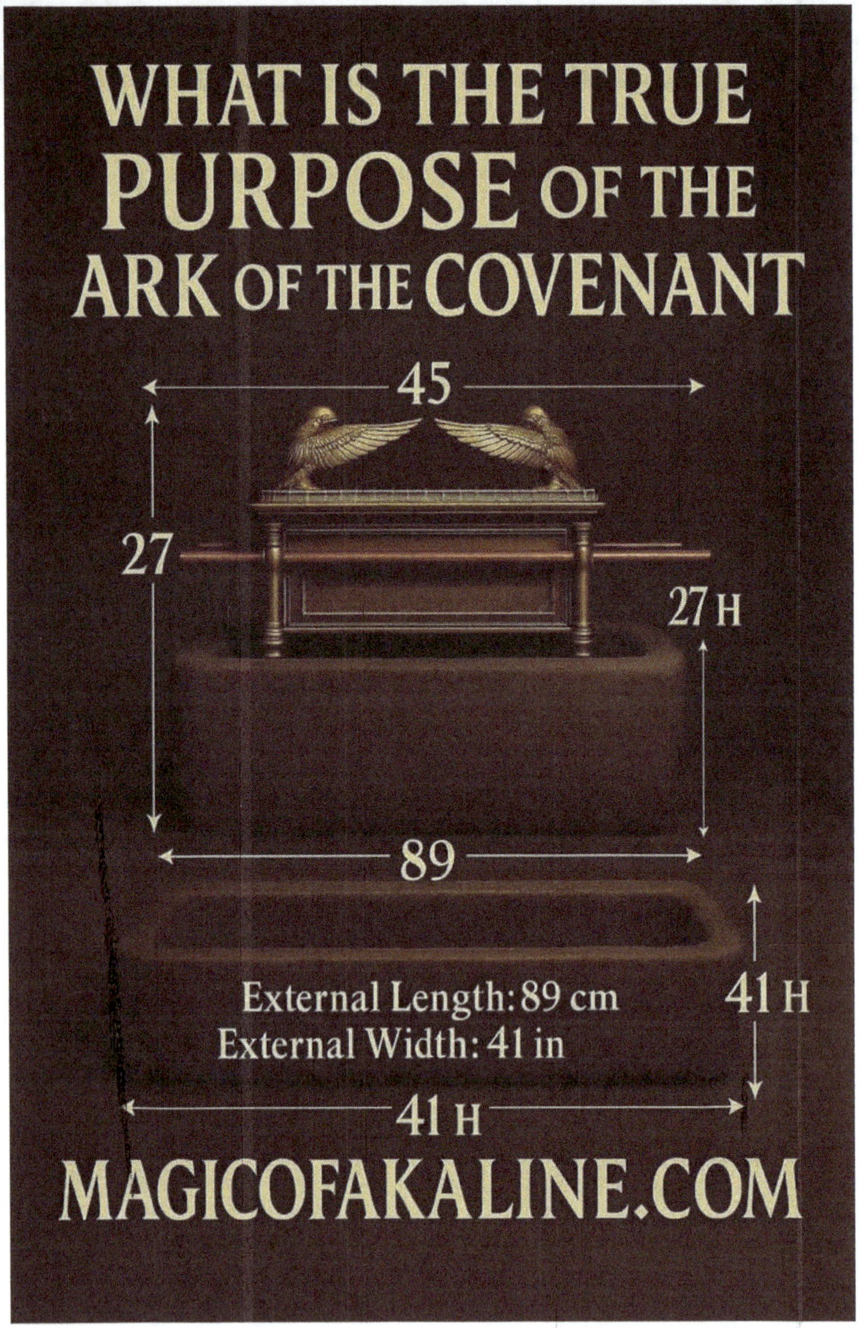
WHAT IS THE TRUE
PURPOSE OF THE
ARK OF THE COVENANT
45
27
27 H
89
External Length: 89 cm
External Width: 41 in
41 H
41 H
MAGICOFAKALINE.COM

The Ark Of The Covenant, Great Pyramid of Giza Connection

Let's journey into the mystery.

<u>The Ark was not just built it was taken.</u>

In Exodus 25:10, God gave Moses precise dimensions for the Ark: two and a half cubits long, a cubit and a half wide, and a cubit and a half high.

But these weren't new numbers.

They were the same proportions already hidden in Egypt, carved into the granite coffer inside the Great Pyramid.

The Ark, it seems, was originally part of the Pyramid's energy system, a golden capacitor resting in the King's Chamber.

Moses, raised in Pharaoh's courts and trained in Egypt's mysteries, knew of this sacred device.

The Exodus: More Than Just Freedom

According to the Book of Exodus, Moses led the Israelites out of Egypt after ten plagues shook the empire. Pharaoh finally let them go — crushed, defeated.

But then…

He changed his mind.

He gathered his entire army and charged after them. Why?

Pride? Anger?

Or did Moses take something Egypt couldn't afford to lose?

The Ark & The Pyramid: A Forbidden Departure

What if Moses didn't just take his people…

What if he took the Ark from the King's Chamber of the Great Pyramid?

The dimensions of the Ark of the Covenant — 2.5 x 1.5 x 1.5 cubits (about 45 x 27 x 27 inches) — match exactly the inner dimensions of the granite sarcophagus still resting inside the King's Chamber of the Great Pyramid of Giza.

Coincidence? Or deliberate design?

What Did the Ark Do?

Biblical texts reveal:

- It parted rivers (Joshua 3:13)
- It crushed enemies (1 Samuel 5:1–12)
- It emitted energy so powerful it could kill instantly (2 Samuel 6:7)

But perhaps most mysteriously…

The Ark may not have been a weapon —

It may have been a power source.

The Great Pyramid: A Massive Water Ionization Reactor?

Modern science now reveals:

- The Great Pyramid is built atop natural underground aquifers
- Eight mysterious wells lie directly beneath the structure
- The pyramid's inner design — including the Grand Gallery and King's Chamber — acts as a hydraulic and acoustic resonator.

If the Ark once sat inside the sarcophagus, it may have completed an ancient energetic system:

→ Creating electromagnetic resonance

→ Inducing electrolysis in underground water

→ Producing highly ionized, micro-clustered alkaline water.

A living elixir.

The Water of Life.

Why Did Pharaoh Really Chase Moses?

With the Ark gone, Egypt's energy field collapsed.

No more resonance.

No more ionized water.

No more anti-aging, elite-exclusive elixir of vitality.

Pharaoh wasn't just losing slaves…

He was losing access to the most powerful life-sustaining force of his empire.

So he chased after it — and was swallowed by the sea.

The Ark, the Temple, and the Water of Life

It doesn't stop there.

• The Holy of Holies in Solomon's Temple shared the same exact volume as the King's Chamber.

• The Ark of the Covenant was the centerpiece in both.

• The Molten Sea on the Temple Mount was filled with sacred water — perhaps ionized.

Across cultures and continents, the same pattern appears:

Ark + Chamber + Water = Life-force Technology

This wasn't religion.

It was science in disguise.

The Technology Returns — Through You

Today, we're rediscovering this ancient technology.

Modern water ionizers, like the state-of-the-art water ionizers featured in Daniel Di-Maios' websites on this landing page, use platinum-coated titanium plates and advanced electrolysis to recreate what the ancients may have mastered:

The 7 Types of Sacred Water:

- Alkaline Water (pH 9.5) – For deep hydration and detoxification
- Clensing Water (pH 4.5–6.0) – Astringent for glowing skin and hair
- Strong Acid Water (pH 2.5) – Powerful disinfectant
- Neutral Water (pH 7.0) – Ideal for medications and infant formula
- Strong Water (pH 11+) – For removing oil-based pesticides
- Clean Water (pH 7.0) – Chlorine-free and fluoride-reduced
- Slightly Alkaline Drinking Water (pH 8.5–9.5) – Everyday wellness

Pharaohs Had It First. Now You Can Too.

They built pyramids to protect it.

They fought wars to reclaim it.

They called it sacred.

Now, you can call it yours.

Unlock the power of ancient wisdom combined with cutting-edge innovation.

Reclaim the Water of Life.

Experience the Secret Pharaohs Took to the Grave.

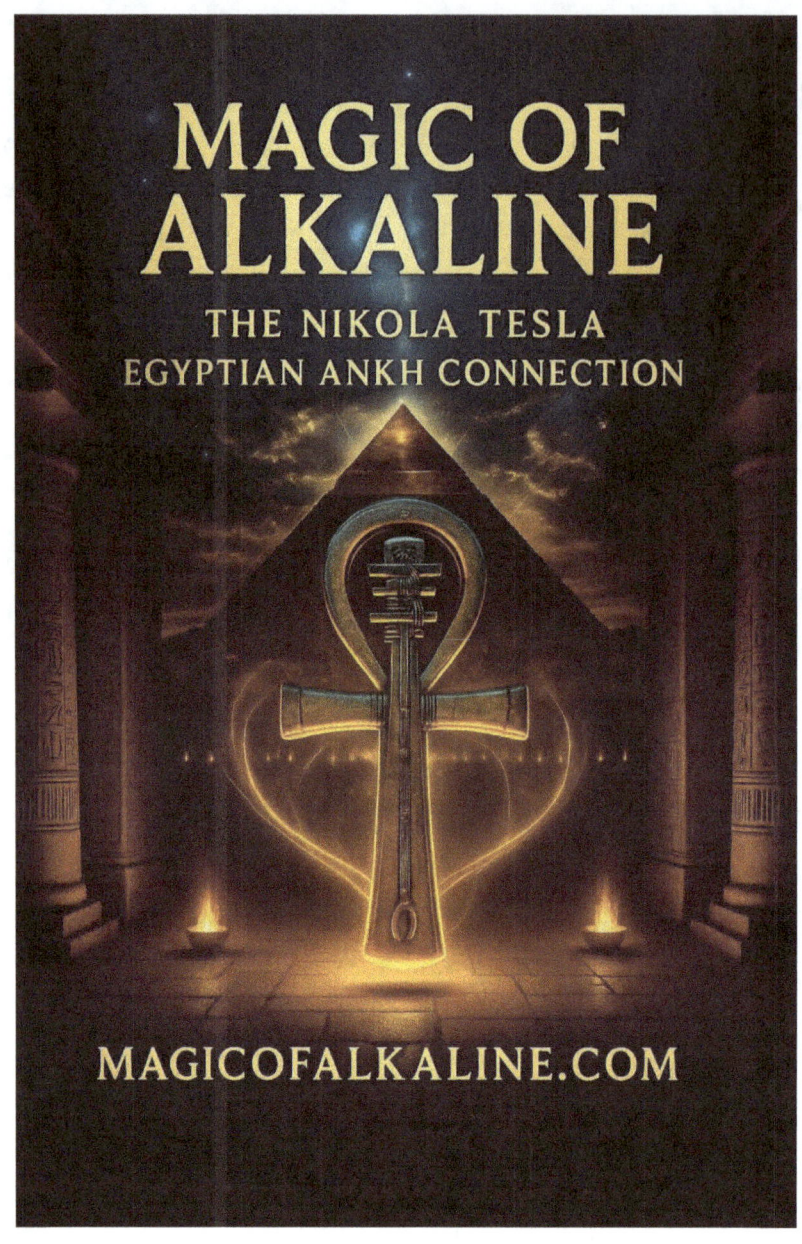

The Nicola Tesla Electric Oscillator Egyptian Ankh Connection

The Water of Life in Every Drop

Modern Water Ionizers are more than a revolutionary device that harmonizes ancient wisdom with cutting-edge science.

By drawing inspiration from the Egyptian Ankh, the symbol of life, and Nikola Tesla's Electric Oscillator, a pioneering invention in energy transformation, water ionizers redefine the way we interact with water, energy, and wellness.

The Egyptian Ankh: Water as the Key to Life

In ancient Egypt, the Ankh represented the essence of life itself.

Often depicted in the hands of gods, it symbolized vitality, divine energy, and the infinite cycle of regeneration.

Water was central to this philosophy, seen as a conduit of life force, essential for both spiritual and physical well-being.

Modern Water Ionizers embody this principle by transforming ordinary water into ionized, hydrogen-rich alkaline water that nourishes the body at a cellular level.

Just as the Ankh channeled divine energy, Daniel Di-Maio's water ionizers enhance the life-giving properties of water, providing hydration that supports longevity, vitality, and overall wellness.

Tesla's Electric Oscillator: Energy in Motion

Nikola Tesla, a visionary of the modern age, developed the Electric Oscillator to generate high-frequency electrical currents, unlocking new ways to transmit and harness energy.

His work was based on the idea that everything in the universe is vibrating energy, including water.

Modern Water Ionizers operate on a similar principle

With the best Water Ionizers having multiple platinum-dipped titanium plates, they efficiently ionize water using advanced electrolysis, restructuring its molecular composition to enhance antioxidant potential, hydrogen content, and bioavailability.

Like Tesla's oscillator, which transformed electrical energy, water ionizers transform water into a highly charged, structured, and optimized form that the body can absorb more efficiently.

Merging the Ancient and the Modern

By bridging the life-affirming power of the Ankh with Tesla's groundbreaking discoveries in energy and frequency, the top-of-the-line water ionizers are more than just a water ionizer; they're a portal to enhanced vitality.

It provides water that rejuvenates, energizes, and harmonizes the body, much like the ancient Egyptians envisioned and as Tesla theorized through his mastery of vibrational energy.

Unlock the Power of Water. Unlock the Power of Life.

With the top of the top-of-the-line water ionizers, every sip is a step toward optimal health, energy, and longevity powered by science, inspired by history, and designed for the future.

What if the "key of life" wasn't just a symbol, but a blueprint hinting that energy and water have always been inseparable?

In the late 1800s, Nikola Tesla demonstrated high-frequency electrical oscillators that produced looping, luminous discharges, shapes that echo the Egyptian ankh's oval and crossbar.

While the visual rhyme is poetic, the practical rhyme is better: oscillating electricity is excellent at energizing systems, and energized water is created every day by a simpler cousin of Tesla's showpiece—electrolysis. [1–3]

Electrolysis uses direct current and specialized electrodes to split water at the surface, producing two streams with distinct characteristics: one more alkaline (rich in hydroxide and dissolved hydrogen), the other more acidic.

Engineers tune voltage, frequency (for rectified/conditioned supplies), electrode materials, and flow paths to influence pH, oxidation-reduction potential (ORP), and dissolved hydrogen content.

The result is ionized, alkalized water on one side and an oxidizing sanitizing stream on the other. [2–6]

Why this matters to the Magic of Alkaline story

• Energy → Structure → Function: Electrochemistry shows that when you supply ordered energy to water, you can restructure the ionic balance (pH, ORP) and separate streams for different purposes.

That engineering mindset is central to our mission and demos at Magic of Alkaline. [2–6]

• Ancient motifs, modern methods: The ankh (symbol of "life") and the carefully aligned geometry of the Great Pyramid invite the idea that form channels energy.

Whether or not ancient works were "machines," the takeaway for today is clear: geometry, materials, and fields change what water can do. Our modern tool is the electrolyzer. [7–10]

• The Ark motif: Biblical descriptions of the Ark of the Covenant emphasize precise dimensions, layered conductive materials, and a dangerous, radiant presence.

 Read symbolically, it's another reminder that controlled fields and careful materials matter.

In modern labs, that's exactly how we design electrolyzers and power supplies for reliable water characteristics. [11–12]

From Tesla's Oscillators to Today's Electrolyzers

Tesla's high-frequency systems weren't designed to make drinking water, but they taught the world how field strength, frequency, and resonance affect gases, plasmas, and surfaces.

Modern water electrolysis borrows the same electrical literacy, only now we optimize current density, electrode overpotential, and mass transport to produce consistent alkaline and acidic streams. [1–6, 13–16]

• Power & control: Stable DC (often conditioned from AC) drives the hydrogen-evolution reaction at the cathode and oxygen-evolution at the anode. [2–4]

• Materials science: Noble-metal coatings or advanced catalysts lower overpotentials and improve efficiency and durability. [3–5, 13–16]

• Outcomes you can measure: pH, ORP, conductivity, and dissolved hydrogen are quantifiable— no mysticism required. We show these in our demo so you can see the numbers for yourself. [2–6]

Our stance

At Magic of Alkaline, we celebrate the wonder of the past while we measure in the present.

Pyramids and arks make for powerful metaphors; electrolysis makes practical water.

Watch the 10-minute demo, see the instruments, and decide with data.

Watch the demo and explore the science.

References

General citations (history/symbolism/primary sources)

1. Tesla, N. Experiments with Alternate Currents of Very High Frequency and Their Application to Methods of Artificial Illumination. (1891 lecture).

2. Ankh. Encyclopaedia Britannica, latest edition.

3. Lehner, M. The Complete Pyramids: Solving the Ancient Mysteries. Thames & Hudson, 1997.

4. Rossi, C. "Geometry and Alignments of the Giza Pyramids," Journal of Archaeological Science (overview essays & museum notes).

5. Exodus 25:10–22 (dimensions and materials of the Ark).

6. Tubb, J. N. The Canaanites. British Museum Press, 1998 (context for Ark traditions).

Peer-reviewed sources (electrochemistry/electrolyzed water)

2. Zeng, K.; Zhang, D. "Recent progress in alkaline water electrolysis for hydrogen production," Progress in Energy and Combustion Science 36 (2010): 307–326.

3. Carmo, M. et al. "A comprehensive review on PEM water electrolysis," International Journal of Hydrogen Energy 38 (2013): 4901–4934.

4. Trasatti, S. "Progress in the understanding of the hydrogen evolution reaction," Journal of Electroanalytical Chemistry 460 (1999): 1–4.

5. Ding, T. et al. "Applications of electrolyzed water in the food industry," Food Control 40 (2014): 79–86.

6. Fukuzaki, S. "Mechanisms of actions of sodium hypochlorite in cleaning and disinfection processes," Biocontrol Science 11 (2006): 147–157.

7. Carmo, M.; Fritz, D.; Mergel, J.; Stolten, D. "Operating conditions and electrode materials for efficient electrolysis," Int. J. Hydrogen Energy 39 (2014): 154–168.

8. Seitz, L. C. et al. "A highly active oxide anode for oxygen evolution in water," Science 353 (2016): 1011–1014.

9. McCrory, C. et al. "Benchmarking hydrogen and oxygen evolution electrocatalysts," J. Am. Chem. Soc. 137 (2015): 4347–4357.

10. Trasatti, S. "Electrochemical water activation: thermodynamic & kinetic aspects," J. Chem. Soc., Faraday Trans. 70 (1974): 132–147.

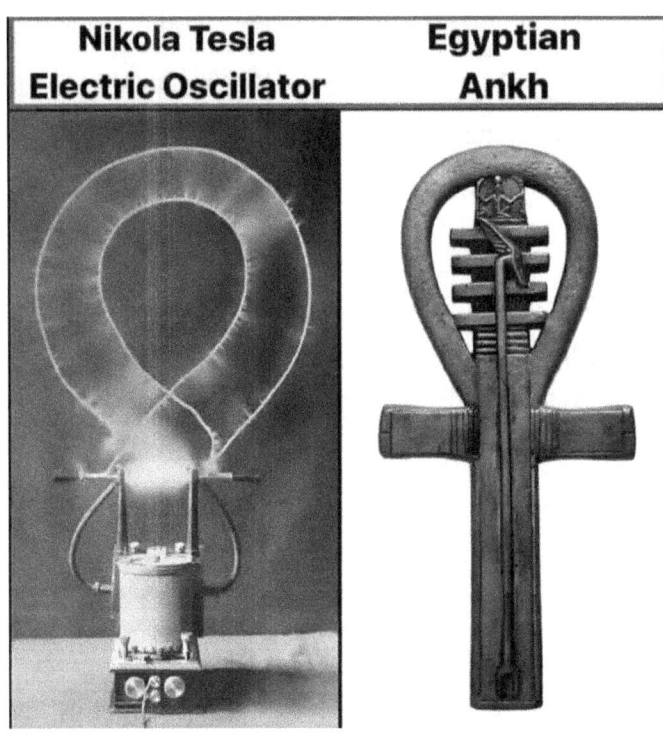

The Staff of Moses Water of Life Connection

The Miracle of Moses, the Ark of the Covenant, and the Power of top-of-the-line Water Ionizers

In Exodus 17:6, Moses, under divine instruction, strikes the rock at Mount Sinai with his staff, miraculously bringing forth water to sustain the Israelites in the wilderness.

This powerful moment symbolizes divine provision, transformation, and the unlocking of life-giving water.

But what if this biblical event also holds a deeper connection to the science of electrolysis, a process central to modern water ionizers?

The Staff, The Ark, and Electrolysis

1. Moses' Staff – The Conductor of Divine Power

• The staff of Moses was more than just a rod; it was a channel for miracles.

From parting the Red Sea to drawing water from the rock, it symbolizes the transmission of energy and transformation, much like the ionization process in top-of-the-line water ionizers.

2. The Ark of the Covenant – A Divine Electrical Force

• The Ark of the Covenant, often associated with divine energy, was said to carry immense power.

Some historians and theorists suggest that it functioned as an ancient capacitor, a vessel storing and discharging energy.

This parallels the electrical charge used in modern water ionizers to separate water into alkaline and acidic streams, creating structured, energized, and antioxidant-rich water.

3. Electrolysis at Mount Sinai?

Imagine the moment Moses struck the rock with his staff—could it have triggered an electrolysis-like reaction?

The rock, possibly containing mineral-rich elements, may have acted as a natural anode, while the force of the strike, combined with divine energy, initiated the separation of water, much like how today's water ionizers transform tap water into molecular hydrogen-rich, ionized water.

Modern Water Ionizers – Bringing the Miracle of Water to Your Home

Top-of-the-line Water Ionizers harness the power of electrolysis, much like the mystical forces at play in biblical times, to transform ordinary water into something extraordinary.

With the Top of the top-of-the-line Water Ionizers having multiple platinum-coated titanium plates, this advanced system:

Energizes and structures water, making it more absorbable.

Produces powerful alkaline water, rich in antioxidants to fight free radicals.

Delivers acidic water for cleansing, just as natural elements purify and restore.

Water of Life – Then and Now

Just as Moses provided water for his people, today, The Best Water Ionizers brings the "Water of Life" to your home, promoting health, vitality, and hydration.

The staff, the Ark, and the miracle at Mount Sinai remind us that water is more than just a drink; it's a gift, a transformation, and a life force.

Experience the power of Ionized Alkalized pH 9.5 water.

The Caduceus Water of Life Connection

Modern Water Ionizers - Modern-Day Caduceus of Water and Life

Water is the source of all life, and in ancient mythology, few symbols embody healing and vitality as powerfully as the Caduceus, the staff entwined with two serpents, often linked to divine wisdom and transformative energy.

Top-of-the-line Water Ionizers continue this legacy, acting as a modern alchemical tool, transforming ordinary water into ionized, antioxidant-rich Ionized Water—the very essence of rejuvenation and vitality.

The Caduceus & Water Ionizers: A Parallel of Healing and Balance

• The Dual Serpents: Representing balance, energy flow, and healing, much like modern water ionizers balance pH levels to restore the body's natural equilibrium.

• Water as Life Force: Just as the Caduceus symbolizes divine medicine, Ionized Water serves as a modern elixir, fueling hydration at the cellular level and aiding in detoxification.

• Electrified Vitality: Top-of-the-Line Water Ionizers employ cutting-edge electrolysis technology, much like the mythical staff channeling cosmic energy, restructuring water into its most bioavailable form for health and longevity.

Water Ionizers: The Ultimate Fountain of Youth

• Top-of-the-line Water Ionizers have multiple Titanium-Coated Platinum Plates: Deliver powerful electrolysis, increasing antioxidant potential and micro-clustering for superior hydration.

• Customizable pH Levels: From alkaline-rich hydration to acidic water, top-of-the-line water ionizers provide versatility for health and wellness.

• Touchscreen Intelligence: A futuristic interface on top-of-the-line Water Ionizers guiding you toward optimal water for every need—like the wisdom passed through sacred symbols.

Transform Your Water. Elevate Your Life.

The best water ionizers aren't just a water machine; they're a key to unlocking the age-old secrets of vitality, balance, and purification.

Experience the Water of Life—Experience The Magic of Alkaline

Was Yahweh a Dragon?

For thousands of years, the image of Yahweh—the God of the Israelites—has been veiled in mystery.

A voice from the mountain, cloaked in fire, smoke, and thunder.

A presence so terrifying that even Moses trembled.

But what if we've misunderstood something critical about this ancient being?

What if Yahweh… was a dragon?

This isn't fantasy.

This is a serious biblical and historical exploration rooted in scripture, archaeology, and ancient tradition.

The Dwelling of Fire

According to the Bible, Yahweh physically dwelt in the tabernacle for 440 years—manifesting as fire, smoke, and terrifying power.

In Deuteronomy 32:22, it is written:

"For a fire is kindled by my anger, and it burns to the depths of Sheol…"

This is not metaphorical.

Over and over again, the text describes a fiery, consuming being.

In Job 41:19-21, we read:

"Out of his mouth go burning lights; sparks of fire shoot out.

Smoke goes out of his nostrils… his breath kindles coals, and a flame goes out of his mouth."

The creature being described here sounds nothing like the tame God of Sunday school—it sounds exactly like a dragon.—

The Sacrifices: Gold, Virgins, and Livestock

In Numbers 31, we encounter one of the Bible's most controversial events.

After defeating the Midianites, the Israelites delivered staggering spoils to Yahweh:

• 337,500 sheep and goats — 675 were Yahweh's portion

• 36,000 cattle — 72 to Yahweh

• 30,500 donkeys — 61 to Yahweh

• 16,000 virgin girls — 32 offered to Yahweh

Also mentioned: 420 pounds of gold collected and presented.

Why does Yahweh desire gold, livestock, and virgin girls?

It's worth noting:

• The Aztecs sacrificed virgin girls to Quetzalcoatl, their feathered serpent god.

• In Japanese Shinto lore, the eight-headed dragon Yamata no Orochi demanded virgin sacrifices.

• Even in early Christian tales like St. George and the Dragon, towns offered up virgin daughters daily to appease the beast.

These parallels are hard to ignore.—

Yahweh and the Serpent

In Numbers 21:6, Yahweh sends "fiery serpents" to punish the Israelites.

In response, He commands Moses to create a serpent idol—a bronze serpent on a pole—and tells the people to worship it to be healed.

This is the only idol Yahweh ever permitted.

Why a serpent? Why copper?

In Isaiah 6:2, the angels (seraphim) are described as "burning ones"—winged, serpent-like beings.

The word "Saraph" means "to burn."

It doesn't just mean angel; it implies a fiery, serpentine being.

The prophet Zechariah (6:1) and Deuteronomy 33:2 describe Yahweh as descending in flame from the mountains of copper—a detail strangely echoed in metallurgical traditions.—

Yahweh vs El: Two Different Gods?

In Deuteronomy 32:8-9, we read something startling:

"When the Most High (El) gave the nations their inheritance… Yahweh's portion was his people."

El and Yahweh are not the same in early texts.

Yahweh was appointed by El as a national deity over Israel.

Later traditions blurred the lines.

But early on, they were separate beings.

2 Enoch 11-12 introduces Chalkydri—winged, copper serpents that surround the throne of El.

Chalkydri literally means "copper serpent."— The Dragon in the Mountain

Everything converges on this one truth:

Yahweh—described with fiery breath, wings, and the thirst for gold, virgin offerings, and sacrifice—matches global dragon archetypes far more than the later spiritualized depictions allow.

And where does Yahweh dwell?

"The Lord came from Sinai… and the mountains quaked at the presence of Yahweh."

(Judges 5:4, Habakkuk 3:3)

He came from the mountain, like a dragon in his lair. And the people trembled.—

Revelation or Reawakening?

This may sound controversial. It should. But if we read the scriptures without modern filters, a shocking image emerges—one that may upend everything we thought we knew.

The ancients weren't writing myths.

They were writing history.

The real question is: Can we handle the truth?—

Stay tuned. The fire has only just begun.

Daniel Di-Maio

magicofalkaline.com

32

Before the Flood — A Different Earth, A Different Water

Imagine standing in a world where the sky glowed with a soft golden light, filtered through a dense water canopy high above the earth.

A world where oxygen was richer, the air was cleaner, and towering trees—two miles high—reached into the heavens like living skyscrapers.

This was the antediluvian Earth described in ancient records, a paradise of perfect balance, vibrant ecosystems, and lifespans measured not in decades, but in centuries.

Everything was bigger, healthier, and more alive… because the water, atmosphere, and energy of the planet were unlike anything we experience today.

The Water of Life

Before the flood, water wasn't simply "wet." It was energized, mineral-rich, and naturally structured by the earth's forces, flowing through pristine aquifers, purified by vast layers of stone, and charged by the planet's magnetic and electrical fields.

This water nourished the colossal plant life, sustained massive animals, and energized the human body in ways modern science is only beginning to rediscover.

Today, most water is a shadow of its former glory, chemically treated, stripped of vitality, and stored in lifeless containers.

But through advanced technology, we can recreate aspects of that pre-flood water: alkaline, ionized, and rich in life-giving properties.

Why It Matters for You

The difference between survival and thriving comes down to the quality of what you put into your body.

Water is your body's primary building material—it fuels every cell, every thought, every heartbeat.

The ancients drank water that amplified life itself.

You deserve to experience the closest thing possible today.

It's time to rediscover what's been lost.

Step into a new chapter of your health and vitality.

Because the water you drink should be as alive as you are.

Magic of Alkaline — In the Time of the Titans

Long before modern history, the earth was ruled by beings of immense size and strength, the Titans, known in the Bible as the giants of old, men of renown (Genesis 6:4).

Their origin was not purely human.

The Book of Enoch reveals that fallen angels descended to earth and mingled with the daughters of men, giving rise to a corrupted race that filled the world with violence and bloodshed.

Because of this corruption, the Creator declared His judgment through the Great Flood of Noah.

The waters poured out from the heavens and burst forth from the deep, covering even the highest mountains of the earth (Genesis 7:19–20).

For forty days and forty nights, the storm raged until the world as it was known was buried beneath the waves.

But the flood was not just rain; it was a force so immense that it altered the face of the earth forever.

The giants, the Titans of old, were swept away and their massive bodies entombed in mud, stone, and sediment.

Over time, these remains became petrified, forming the very rock formations we see today.

Look closely at the cliffs, mountains, and islands across the world.

Look at the Mother elephant and her baby facing each other, frozen in time after being overtaken by the floodwaters.

Shapes of human faces, bodies, and even great beasts are frozen in stone.

These are not mere accidents of erosion, but silent witnesses of the judgment described in Scripture.

The mountains themselves cry out, telling us the truth of the Flood.

The Book of Enoch records this moment with haunting clarity: the Watchers who sinned were bound, their offspring destroyed, and the world was cleansed by water.

Genesis echoes this same story, reminding us that the Flood was not just a local event, but a worldwide act of cleansing and renewal.

Today, the petrified Titans remain as evidence.

They stand like monuments to the truth of God's Word, a truth written not only in Scripture but carved into the very bones of the earth.

The Flood was real.

The Titans were real.

And the rocks themselves still testify.

In The Age of The Titans

An origin story for Magic of Alkaline about wonder, water, and a world that once was bigger, way bigger!

Picture a brilliant, gold-washed morning: three unimaginable trees crown the horizon; two miles tall, living "titans" roam a green world carved by rivers, lakes, and inland seas.

That's the spirit of our artwork and the spirit of Magic of Alkaline.

We celebrate water's power to shape worlds, nourish life, and inspire awe.

Before the Flood—how the world really differed

Even within human prehistory, Earth looked strikingly different.

During the last ice age, sea level stood roughly 120–130 meters lower than today, exposing vast coastal plains and changing where rivers met the sea.

As ice sheets melted, sea level rose rapidly in pulses, catastrophic by human standards, remaking shorelines and river valleys across the planet.

Some floods were sudden and colossal.

Geologists have mapped enormous "megaflood" landscapes (e.g., the Channeled Scablands in the American Northwest) formed when glacial lakes burst, releasing volumes of water rivaling the world's largest rivers in a matter of days.

Far from myth alone, regional cataclysms also struck coastlines.

A leading hypothesis proposes a dramatic, late-glacial Black Sea inundation when Mediterranean water surged through the Bosporus, rapidly drowning shelf landscapes that had been dry only years before.

And meltwater pulses were global.

One well-documented episode (Meltwater Pulse 1A, ~14,600 years ago) raised seas by several meters in mere centuries, an extraordinary rate compared with modern change.

Water in the world's oldest sky

Ancient Near Eastern peoples pictured a sky-dome with "waters above"—a cultural cosmology echoed in Genesis.

Whether or not one reads those lines literally, the image captures how foundational people understood water to be: it framed the world from firmament to fountains.

"Titans," scale, and living memory

The late Pleistocene teemed with megafauna: mammoths, giant ground sloths, and enormous bison.

Their presence (and rapid disappearance) transformed ecosystems and surely human storytelling.

Our "titans" draw on that sense of scale: creatures large enough to make a person feel very small.

What this means for the Magic of Alkaline

Our name nods to a simple truth: water is elemental.

From ice-age rivers powerful enough to move mountains to the mineral springs that buffer pH and shape taste, water's chemistry and motion are inseparable from life.

We don't claim miracle cures; we do honor the craft of clean, mineral-balanced drinking water, because the way water moves through rock, soil, and air is part of its "magic."

Our ethos

- Reverence: Water shaped the "Age of Titans"; it still shapes us.

- Respect for science & story: We pair mythic imagination with peer-reviewed research.

- Care for quality: Thoughtful mineral balance and great taste—water you'll love to drink.

Sources & further reading

- Seely, P. H. "The Firmament and the Water Above (Part I & II)." Westminster Theological Journal 53–54 (1991–92).

- Lambeck, K., et al. "Sea level and global ice volumes from the Last Glacial Maximum to the Holocene." PNAS 111 (2014): 15296–15303.

- Deschamps, P., et al. "Ice-sheet collapse and sea-level rise at the Bølling warming 14,600 years ago." Nature 483 (2012): 559–564.

- Ryan, W. B. F., et al. "An abrupt drowning of the Black Sea shelf." Marine Geology 138 (1997): 119–126.

- Baker, V. R. "The Channeled Scabland: A Retrospective." Annual Review of Earth and Planetary Sciences 37 (2009): 393–411.

- Gregoire, L. J., et al. "Abrupt Bølling warming and ice-shelf collapse inferred from freshwater discharge." PNAS 113 (2016): 1074–1079.

- Condron, A., & Winsor, P. "Meltwater routing and the Younger Dryas." PNAS 109 (2012): 19928–19933.

- Koch, P. L., & Barnosky, A. D. "Late Quaternary extinctions: State of the debate." Annual Review of Ecology, Evolution, and Systematics 37 (2006): 215–250.

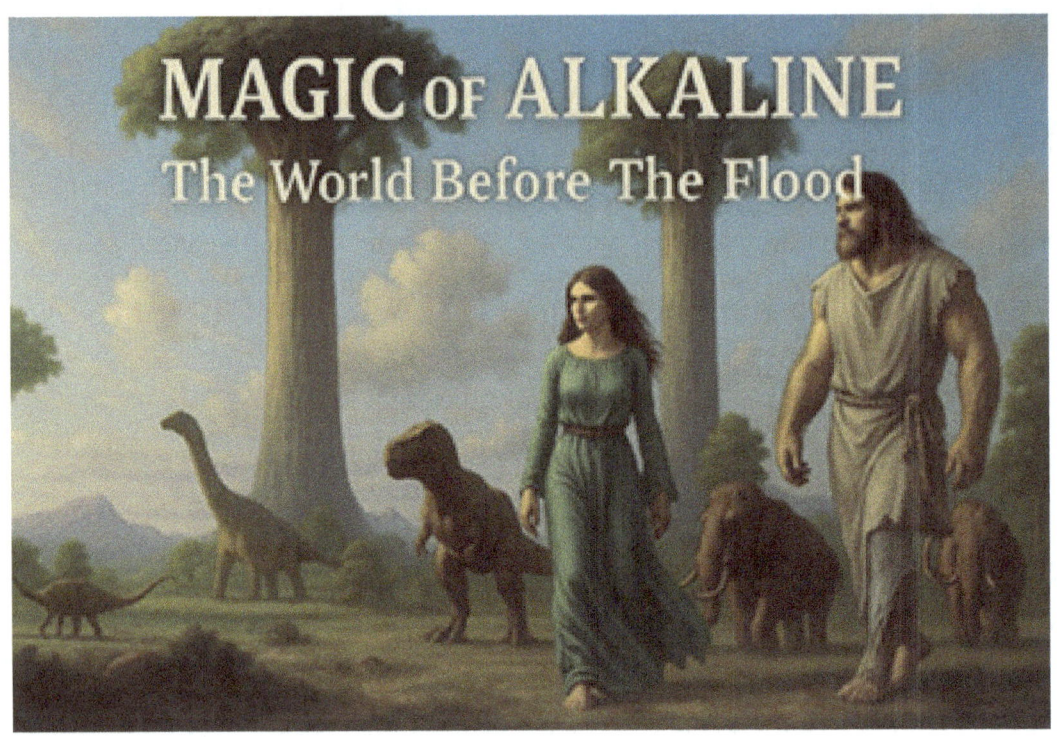

MAGIC OF ALKALINE
IN THE TIME OF THE TITAN'S
magicofalkaline.com

The World Before The Flood

The Forgotten World Before the Flood

Long before written history, there was a time when the world pulsed with power and life unlike anything we see today.

This was the Andaluvian Age, the time before the great flood, a world where air was thicker, oxygen richer, and the Earth itself hummed with vitality.

Here, vast trees stretched two miles into the sky, their trunks so wide that villages could have lived inside them.

Dinosaurs roamed freely, not as creatures of museums but as part of a living, breathing ecosystem.

And among them walked the Titans, giant men and women of unparalleled strength and stature otherwise known in the Bible as (The Nephlem).

Even more astonishing, regular people lived alongside these giants, aka Nephlem, small in comparison yet sharing the same valleys, rivers, and skies.

All beings, great and small, were bound by one unifying force: the water that sustained them.

Titans & Trees: Giants Among Giants

The Titans were not legends then; they were neighbors, leaders, hunters, and guardians.

Their enormous frames were nourished by food that grew larger, air that carried more energy, and most importantly, water charged with life.

The giant trees, rising higher than modern skyscrapers, drew water from deep underground aquifers.

These ancient root systems filtered and energized water until it was more than simple hydration; it was living electricity, carrying minerals, ions, and vibrational frequencies.

This water coursed through the land, nourishing not only the Titans but everything in creation.

Dinosaurs & Waterways: Colossal Beasts Sustained

Dinosaurs, too, depended on this extraordinary water.

The brontosaurus, grazing under the shadow of trees that dwarfed even its massive neck, thrived because of streams infused with Earth's elemental balance.

The Tyrannosaurus Rex, though fierce, was no enemy of the Titans, merely another creature in the grand design of this shared ecosystem.

Water bound them all together. Without it, such massive bodies and ecosystems would have collapsed. With it, they endured for ages.

Regular People in a Giant's World

But what of mankind as we know it, the smaller men and women, much like us today?

They lived alongside the Titans, learning to adapt, to thrive, and to honor the sources of life.

Though dwarfed in size, these early people were not insignificant.

They witnessed the strength of Titans, the grandeur of dinosaurs, and the majesty of the trees, and they knew the secret was not merely in size or strength. The secret was always in the water.

The Lost Chemistry of Water

The water of the Andaluvian Age was not what flows from taps today.

It was mineral-rich, electrically charged, alkaline, and ionized by nature itself.

Flowing through rock, infused with Earth's energy, and resonating with natural frequencies, it sustained life at scales unimaginable today.

When the great flood reshaped the Earth, much of this ecosystem was buried, altered, and hidden.

What we drink now is only a faint shadow of that original, vital water.

Rediscovering Ancient Power Today

Here at Magic of Alkaline, we believe that water is more than hydration.

It is memory, energy, and vitality.

Modern technology allows us to rediscover what the Titans and the ancients once knew:

That water can be restored to its living state.

When you drink ionized alkaline water, you are not just quenching thirst; you are connecting to a forgotten age when Titans walked, dinosaurs roared, and the Earth overflowed with life.

This is not fantasy. This is a remembered truth.

Conclusion: A Glass Into the Lost World

Every glass of alkaline water is a doorway into that time, the era when humanity, Titans, dinosaurs, and colossal trees thrived together.

By restoring water to its original vitality, we step back into alignment with the Earth as it was meant to be.

The magic of Alkaline isn't about nostalgia for the past.

It's about carrying forward the strength, vitality, and harmony of that forgotten world—into your body, your life, and your future.

The Flood

The Age Before the Waters Rose

The ancient world before the Great Flood was unlike anything we know today.

The Bible tells us in Genesis 6 that the "sons of God" descended and mingled with humankind, giving rise to the Nephilim, giant beings of great stature and power.

Other texts banned from the Bible, such as The Book of Enoch and The Book of Giants, expand on this story, revealing how these fallen angels and their offspring corrupted creation itself, altering animals, plants, and mankind.

It was a time when Titan creatures roamed the Earth, animals so immense they dwarfed modern species.

The land was dotted with forests of colossal trees that stretched miles into the sky, their canopies forming the very architecture of Edenic life.

This was the world that God judged with the Flood.

The Titan Animals and Their Fate

As the waters began to rise, the very size of the Titan animals became their doom.

Mud and torrential rains created a trap.

Their massive feet sank into the ground, and when the walls of water came upon them, they drowned where they stood.

Today, this is why we find mud fossilized Titan creatures, frozen in their final moments, petrified in stone.

The records—both fossil and textual—tell us of at least twelve types of Titan animals:

1. Titan Elephants – over 30 feet tall, with tusks the length of ships' masts.

2. Titan Rhinoceroses – plated like walking fortresses.

3. Titan Horses – towering above men like moving towers of muscle.

4. Titan Lions – kings of the land, with paws the size of shields.

5. Titan Wolves – packs that roamed like storms.

6. Titan Bears – so great they could uproot trees.

7. Titan Birds – wingspans stretching across valleys.

8. Titan Boars – tusks like spears, bodies like armored wagons.

9. Titan Serpents – dragons of the earth, swallowing livestock whole.

10. Titan Crocodiles – river beasts longer than ships.

11. Titan Mammoths – shaggy towers, echoing the elephants but even greater.

12. Titan Fish – sea monsters that prowled the deep, recorded in both Genesis and Enoch as "Leviathan."

Each perished in the same way: trapped in the mud, overtaken by the waters, preserved in stone as a testimony to a world judged.

The Cutting of the Giant Trees

Another mystery of the Flood comes from the giant tree stumps still scattered across our planet.

In the Book of Enoch and Jubilees, we are told of angels sent by God to bring judgment.

Part of their mission was to cut down the great trees, so immense that they reached to the heavens, so that the Titan people could not climb them to escape the deluge.

These were not trees as we know them, but living skyscrapers, organic mountains of wood.

When cut, their stumps remained, scattered across Earth, mistaken today for mesas and plateaus. The most famous example is Devil's Tower in Wyoming, a perfect hexagonal trunk, once the body of a tree stretching miles high.

Other known giant tree stumps include:

1. Devils Tower – Wyoming, USA

2. Uluru – Australia

3. Giant's Causeway – Ireland

4. Table Mountain – South Africa

5. Mount Roraima – Venezuela/Brazil border

6. Auyán-tepui – Venezuela

7. Sugarloaf Mountain – Brazil

8. Mt. Tai – China

9. My Sinai - Egypt (Not Saudi Arabia)

Each of these carries the scars of having once been alive, their petrified "roots" and perfect geometric patterns echoing the handiwork of a world before the Flood.

Why the Flood Was Necessary

The Bible makes it clear: the Flood was not only a punishment, but a purification.

In Genesis 6:5-7, God saw that the wickedness of man was great upon the Earth, and that every imagination of the thoughts of his heart was only evil continually.

The Nephilim, the hybrid offspring, and the corrupted Titan animals had poisoned creation itself.

The Book of Jubilees and The Book of Enoch explain that the fallen angels had taught men sorcery, war, and blood sacrifice.

The giants devoured both animals and humans, bringing violence without end.

Creation was in ruin.

Thus, the Flood was a reset.

By cutting down the giant trees, drowning the Titan animals, and cleansing the Earth with water, God restored the balance of creation.

Only Noah, his family, and the preserved animals within the Ark survived to repopulate the world in purity.

The Legacy of the Flood

When we look at fossilized Titan creatures, when we see tree-stump mountains like Devils Tower, when we read the fragments of Enoch and the tales of the Nephilim, we are staring at the evidence of a forgotten world.

The Flood was more than myth; it was history, recorded in stone, scripture, and the scars of our planet.

It was the day the heavens wept, the waters rose, and God reset the balance of life.

References for THE FLOOD

1. The Age Before the Waters Rose

• Biblical References

• Genesis 6:1–4 — "The sons of God came in to the daughters of men… There were giants (Nephilim) in the earth in those days."

• Genesis 6:11–12 — "The earth also was corrupt before God, and the earth was filled with violence."

• Non-Biblical References

• 1 Enoch 6–7 — Angels (the Watchers) descended on Mount Hermon, took wives, and begot giants.

• The Book of Giants (Dead Sea Scrolls fragment, Qumran) — Describes the massive size of the Nephilim and their destructive violence.

• Jubilees 5:1–11 — Expands on Genesis, noting how the angels defiled creation and God determined to destroy everything with the Flood.—

2. The Titan Animals and Their Fate

• Biblical References

• Job 40:15–24 — Behemoth, a massive beast likened to an elephant or sauropod-like creature.

• Job 41 — Leviathan, a sea monster, "king over all the children of pride."

• Genesis 7:21–23 — "All flesh died that moved upon the earth, both of fowl, and of cattle, and of beast, and of every creeping thing."

• Non-Biblical References

• 1 Enoch 7:3–6 — Giants devoured animals, men, birds, reptiles, and fish, corrupting all flesh.

• Jasher 4:18 (Book of Jasher, cited in Joshua 10:13 and 2 Samuel 1:18, but not in the canon) — All creatures "corrupted their ways and their orders, and began to devour one another."

• The Book of Giants — Mentions beasts created and destroyed during this period.

(This provides backing for naming Titan Elephants, Mammoths, Crocodiles, Serpents, etc., as giant corrupted beasts.)—

3. The Cutting of the Giant Trees

• Biblical References

• Genesis 6:17 — God declares He will "bring a flood of waters upon the earth, to destroy all flesh." While not specific to trees, it sets the judgment context.

• Ezekiel 31:3–18 — References the "cedar of Lebanon" as a metaphor for a cosmic, world-tree so tall that "all the fowls of heaven made their nests in its boughs." Its fall by divine decree mirrors the myth of giant trees being cut down.

• Non-Biblical References

• 1 Enoch 10:4–9 — God commands the archangels (Raphael, Gabriel, Michael) to execute judgment, binding the angels and giants, and destroying their works. Some interpretations say this includes cutting the trees they could have climbed.

• Jubilees 5:6–10 — Details angels being sent to execute judgment upon creation.

• Mythic Parallel: Sumerian, Aztec, and Norse myths all contain "world tree" destruction stories connected with divine judgment (Yggdrasil, Ceiba, etc.).

(This supports the imagery of Devil's Tower and other formations as ancient tree stumps.)—

4. Locations of Giant Tree Stumps

• Main Examples & Interpretive Parallels

1. Devils Tower (Wyoming, USA) — Hexagonal basalt columns resembling giant petrified wood fibers.

2. Uluru (Ayers Rock, Australia) — Sacred sandstone monolith, often linked to world-tree legends.

3. Giant's Causeway (Ireland) — Interlocking basalt columns resembling crystallized tree roots.

4. Table Mountain (South Africa) — Flat-topped "stump-like" formation.

5. Mount Roraima (Venezuela/Brazil) — A Plateau rising sheer like a massive stump.

6. Auyán-tepui (Venezuela) — Known as the "House of the Gods," a towering flat-topped mesa.

7. Sugarloaf Mountain (Brazil) — Dome-like granite peak resembling the top of a stump.

8. Mount Tai (China) — Ancient sacred mountain, mythically tied to heaven and earth connections.

9. Mount Sinai (Egypt) — Though biblically known for the Ten Commandments, its mesa-like shape evokes "cut down tree" imagery.—

5. Why the Flood Was Necessary

• Biblical References

• Genesis 6:5–7 — "The LORD saw that the wickedness of man was great in the earth… I will destroy man whom I have created."

• Genesis 6:13 — "The end of all flesh has come before me; for the earth is filled with violence."

• Genesis 7:11–12 — Waters of the deep broken up, floodgates of heaven opened.

• 2 Peter 2:4-5 — Angels who sinned were cast into chains of darkness; Noah is spared.

• Jude 1:6 7 — Angels left their estate, are held for judgment; parallels Genesis 6.

• Non-Biblical References

• 1 Enoch 9–10 — Angels cry out against the Watchers; God sends archangels to bind them and unleash the Flood.

• Jubilees 5:1–11 — The sins of mankind and giants prompt God to wipe them out with the Flood.

• The Book of Giants — Giants confess their dreams of impending destruction by floodwaters.

Machinery Palace
Pan American Exposition, Butalo 10

Tower of jewels
Panama Pacific Exposition, 1915

WHO BUILT THE PYRAMIDS
AND THESE INCREDIBLE PALACES

MAGICOFALKALINE.COM

Court of Honor
World's Columian Exposit, Chicago 1893

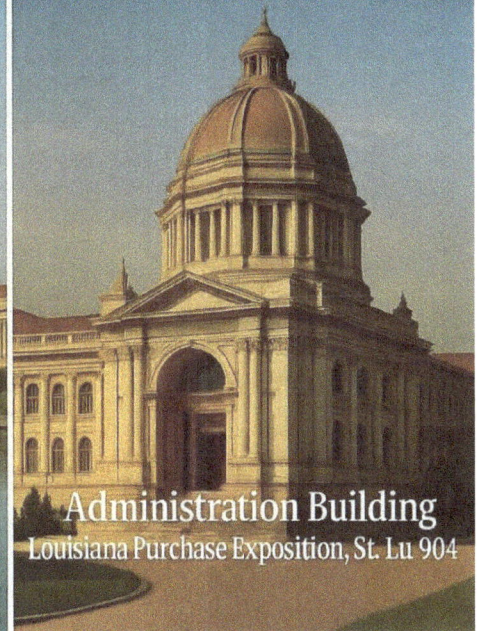

Administration Building
Louisiana Purchase Exposition, St. Lu 904

How Did They Build These Structures... Without Power Tools, Cranes, or Trucks?

Let's look at the facts.

Court of Honor – 1893

Machinery Palace – 1901

Administration Building – 1904

Tower of Jewels – 1915

Keep in mind, these are just four of the hundreds of palaces all over the Earth!!!

All of these grand architectural marvels were allegedly constructed at a time when:

— There were no power tools.

— No diesel trucks to haul 100-ton stone blocks.

— No cranes to lift 20+ ton keystones 10+ stories into the air.

— No electric welding equipment.

— No hydraulic systems.

— And barely any modern concrete.

So how did they do it?

What exactly did they have?

A few horses.

Some donkeys.

A handful of hand chisels.

Wooden carts with iron wheels.

And long, arduous travel routes with zero highway infrastructure.

Yet somehow…

They built massive stone and marble palaces with columns so perfect, even today's laser-cut tech would blush.

They carved exquisite statues, poured enormous domes, and built reflecting pools that still ripple with precision.

And they did it all in less than a year or two.

Meanwhile, in 2025, with access to AI, bulldozers, cranes, CAD software, robotic arms, and 3D laser scanning…

We can't even build a city hall without it looking like a soulless cement shoebox.

Have we evolved backward?

We spend billions on hospitals and schools that look like prisons.

We build skyscrapers that sway in the wind, but crumble after 40 years.

No detail.

No elegance.

No soul.

The buildings of the past whisper secrets.

The question is — do you have ears to hear them?

What ancient energy powered these projects?

What kind of water did these builders drink?

What knowledge has been buried… hidden from the public eye?

It's time to WAKE UP.

Discover the real story behind energy, structure, and the water of life.

 Learn why the ancients weren't primitive — but perhaps more advanced than we are today.

We didn't build these masterpieces. We just inherited the ruins.

The truth is waiting. But not forever.

EGYPTIAN GLYPHS vs. REAL ELONGATED SKULLS
Aliens? Or Older People Whom Lived Longer??
MAGICOFALKALINE.COM

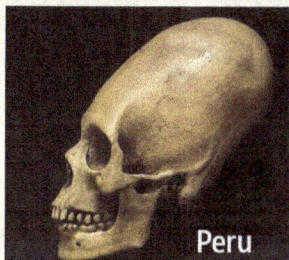
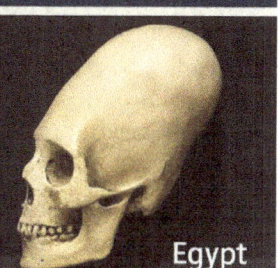
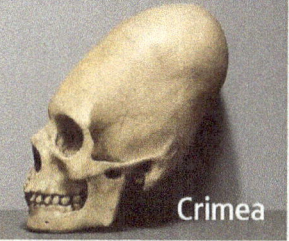
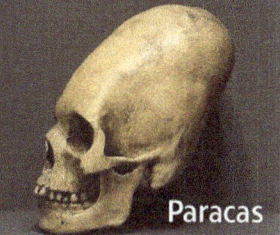

Aliens? Or Older People Whom Lived Longer??

The Secret They Don't Want You to Know

Why Do Egyptian Hieroglyphs Show People with ELONGATED SKULLS…

And Why Are Matching Skulls Found in Egypt, Peru, Crimea, and Beyond?

ALIENS? OR HUMANS WHO LIVED WAY, WAY LONGER THAN WE?

You're not supposed to ask this question.

You're definitely not supposed to find the answer.

But here it is:

The skulls in ancient Egyptian glyphs match elongated skulls found all over the world — from Peru to Crimea, from Paracas to the very sands of Giza.

And here's what mainstream science won't tell you:

HUMAN SKULLS DON'T STOP GROWING.

It's called appositional growth — the cranial bones thicken and elongate with age.

The sutures (the "cracks") of your skull fuse tighter, your jaw enlarges, and your facial features expand over time.

This is well-documented in medical science:

 Source: Gray's Anatomy (1918 edition)

– "The cranial vault bones continue to remodel throughout life via appositional growth."

So What Happens If Someone Lived 200… 400… 1,000 Years?

Their skull would look nothing like ours.

It would be longer.

Heavier.

Massively more developed.

Just like the skulls found in Paracas, Egypt, and Shanidar.

 "Alien Skulls"? Or Just Humans Who Lived for Centuries?

These elongated skulls are not artifacts of binding. Many have:

• No cranial suture lines (indicating non-deformed, natural growth)

• 30% larger cranial volume

• Completely different bone density and structure.

 Source: Dr. Brien Foerster – "The Enigma of Cranial Deformation" (2012)

"Some of these skulls, particularly in Paracas, show no signs of binding — they are naturally elongated. DNA testing reveals mutations unknown in modern humans."

AND HERE'S THE KICKER...

Many of these skulls show life spans FAR longer than ours.

In studies done on osteological development and cranial bone maturity, the age at death for several of these elongated skull specimens is estimated to be:

200 to 400+ years.

Source: Lloyd Pye, "Everything You Know Is Wrong" (2007)

Foerster & L.A. Marzulli, "The Watchers" (2014)

Analysis by Peruvian Anthropologist Dr. Julio Tello

These weren't freaks of nature.

They were likely a class of elite humans, possibly with advanced energy knowledge, living hundreds of years longer due to their environment, water, and electromagnetic surroundings.

Just like… the Pharaohs of Egypt.

Just like… the figures carved in temple walls with elongated heads.

So, What Does This Have to Do with the Magic of Alkaline?

Everything!

The quality of your water, your body's pH, and your electrical energy are directly tied to longevity.

Ancient cultures revered structured, living water – possibly the same kind of water we now rediscover through ionization and electrolysis.

The skulls… the pyramids… the glyphs…

It wasn't just art.

It was a message across time.

And now – you've found the missing link.

Unlock the Real Secret of Longevity

Watch the Shocking Demo Video Now

WATCH THE DEMO

SEE THE COMPENSATION PLAN

LEARN WHY ALKALINE WATER IS THE FUTURE

Final Thought:

If skulls never stop growing…

And we've found skulls that look like they've grown for hundreds of years…

Then maybe the real question is:

Why aren't we living like that anymore?

Take Advantage of this knowledge immediately.

Before this knowledge is buried again._

SACRED SECRETION & THE WATER OF LIFE

Activate the Christ Oil. Illuminate the Pineal. Awaken the Divine Within.

Genesis 32:30 | Matthew 6:22

For thousands of years, ancient mystics, sages, and prophets have spoken of the sacred secretion, the anointing oil, the "Christos," that rises through the spinal column during peak spiritual states.

In scripture, Jacob calls this place Peniel (Genesis 32:30), symbolically referencing the pineal gland—the "single eye" Jesus refers to in Matthew 6:22.

What Is the Sacred Secretion?

The sacred secretion, sometimes called the Christ oil or "Chrism", is described as a bio-spiritual substance created monthly in the body.

Ancient esoteric traditions taught that when conserved and elevated through fasting, prayer, and purity, it travels up the spinal column (Sushumna) and activates the pineal gland.

• Egyptians symbolized it in the Eye of Horus and associated it with the anointing oils of their priests.

• Early Christians referred to it as the "Christos," the anointing of the Holy Spirit (1 John 2:27).

• Eastern Yogic traditions identified it with ojas and amrita, the "nectar of immortality" distilled through discipline and meditation.

• Medieval alchemists sought it in the "Philosopher's Stone," a symbol of inner transmutation.

The Sacred Secretion in Modern Times

Practicing this discipline today

Today, this ancient teaching has resurfaced among seekers, wellness practitioners, and even cultural elites. In fact:

• Neuroscientists confirm that the pineal gland regulates melatonin and may produce DMT, often called the "spirit molecule," linked to mystical visions 【Carhart-Harris et al., Frontiers in Psychology, 2014】.

• Modern holistic practitioners describe the secretion as a biochemical bridge between hormones, neurotransmitters, and spiritual awakening.

• Hollywood and cultural elites, from actors to musicians, openly reference pineal activation, "third eye" symbolism, and sacred oils in music videos, films, and interviews.

These motifs often appear as eyes, pyramids, and serpents in pop culture, echoing ancient esoteric knowledge 【Partridge, The Re-Enchantment of the West, 2005】.

While some pursue synthetic shortcuts, the original path of the sacred secretion emphasizes purification, water, and alignment with divine order.

Practicing the Sacred Secretion Today

1. Understand the Timing

• The secretion is believed to be released once a month, about 2–3 days after the moon enters your sun sign.

• This is sometimes called your "birth cycle" — when your body produces a small amount of "Christ oil" (biochemical essence).

• Knowing your astrological sign and tracking moon phases helps you pinpoint when to practice (e.g., Aries rising in Aries moon).

Reference: Genesis 1:14 — "Let them be for signs, and for seasons, and for days, and years."

2. Purify the Vessel (Body as Temple)

The secretion rises only in a pure, hydrated body:

• Water: Drink ionized alkaline water (pH ~9.5) daily to keep fluids conductive. Hydration is key.

• Diet:

• Minimize processed foods, alcohol, caffeine, and heavy meats during your sacred week.

• Focus on fruits, vegetables, seeds, and high-water-content foods (cucumber, melon, citrus).

• Fasting: Many traditions recommend intermittent fasting (sunrise-to-sunset or 16:8 cycles) to reduce digestive energy drain.

Reference: Daniel 1:12 — "Give us nothing but vegetables to eat and water to drink."

3. Practice Sexual Energy Conservation

• In esoteric Christian, Taoist, and Yogic teachings, ejaculation/orgasm disperses this "oil."

• Practice conservation for at least 3–7 days before and after your moon cycle so the oil is not lost, but preserved and transmuted upwards.

• Women may align this with their hormonal cycles, focusing on ovulation phases and inner stillness.

1 Corinthians 6:19 — "Your body is a temple of the Holy Spirit."

4. Breathwork (Raise the Oil Up the Spine)

The secretion must travel from the sacrum (sacral chakra) → up the spine → to the pineal gland (third eye).

• Spinal Breathing: Sit upright, inhale deeply while visualizing energy moving up the spine, exhale while holding it in the head.

• Alternate Nostril Breathing (Pranayama): Balances the hemispheres of the brain and calms the nervous system.

• Kundalini Breath: Short rhythmic breaths while engaging the diaphragm, visualizing golden oil rising.

5. Meditation & Pineal Activation

• Focused Gaze: Close eyes, roll gaze gently upward toward the point between the eyebrows (third eye).

• Chanting / Vibration: Use sacred sounds ("OM," "Christos," or Psalms) to vibrate the skull cavity and stimulate the pineal.

• Visualization: Imagine a golden oil (light) rising and anointing the pineal gland, illuminating the inner "temple."

Matthew 6:22 — "If thine eye be single, thy whole body shall be full of light."

6. Sacred Secretion Ritual Flow (Practical Daily Routine)

Morning (Sunrise):

• Drink a glass of ionized water.

• 10–20 minutes spinal breathing & meditation.

• Light stretching or yoga postures to stimulate spinal fluid flow.

Afternoon:

• Eat lightly, mostly fruits/vegetables.

• Stay hydrated with structured/ionized water.

• Avoid overstimulation (social media, toxins, sexual release).

Evening (Before Sleep):

• Meditate in silence or prayer.

• Pineal focus: upward gaze, chant, or scripture recitation.

• Sleep early (pineal gland secretes melatonin & possible DMT in deep rest).

7. Integration

• Journal your dreams, visions, or heightened awareness during this time.

• Many report increased intuition, clarity, and even mystical insights.

• Over months of consistent practice, vitality and inner light increase.

Summary for practicing the Sacred Secretion or the "Chrism":

Practicing the sacred secretion today = hydration + purity + conservation + breath + meditation during your moon cycle. When aligned, the Christ oil rises, activating the pineal gland, leading to spiritual illumination — the "anointing" described in scripture.

Why the Sacred Secretion Requires Living Water

Here's what most modern seekers overlook:

• The body cannot complete the sacred secretion process if it's dehydrated, acidic, or toxic.

• Without living water, ionized, negatively charged, high pH water—your temple (body) cannot activate its divine technology.

Why You Need Ionized Alkaline Water (The Water of Life)

Drinking pH 9.5 ionized alkaline water isn't just about physical health—it's about spiritual conductivity.

This water is:

• Rich in negative ions (which reduce oxidative stress)

• Highly hydrating (micro-clustered water penetrates cells deeper)

• Alkalizing, flushing out acidic waste that blocks energy channels

• Alive with bioelectric potential, supporting nervous system activation

• Free from toxic chemicals found in most municipal tap and bottled waters

The Spiritual Link: From Water to Light

As the sacred secretion (Christ oil) journeys from the sacral chakra up the spine (Sushumna), it passes energy centers (chakras) and reaches the pineal gland—if the vessel is pure.

To support this internal ascent, your body must be electrically and vibrationally aligned.

That's where ionized water plays a pivotal role:

"The body is 99% water at the molecular level.

The quality of water determines the quality of consciousness."

— Dr. Masaru Emoto

10 Cited Sources Supporting Ionized Alkaline Water

1. Wright, R.G. Killing Cancer, Not People — alkaline, ionized water and bioelectric balance.

2. Shinya, H. The Enzyme Factor — gut health improved with ionized water.

3. Journal of Biological Chemistry (158.3) — hydration and ATP synthesis.

4. BMC Complementary Medicine & Therapies (2017) — antioxidant properties of ionized water.

5. NASA hydration research — structured water and cellular uptake.

6. Journal of Applied Physiology (2004) — hydration improves brain function.

7. Pollack, G. The Fourth Phase of Water.

8. PubMed (2012) — microclustering effect of ionized water.

9. Asian Pacific Journal of Cancer Prevention (2012)   alkaline water inhibits cancer cell growth.

10. Environmental Health Perspectives (2011) — fluoride and chlorine calcify the pineal gland.

What Happens When You Combine the Sacred Secretion with the Water of Life?

• Increased vitality

• Sharper intuition and mental clarity

• Improved hormonal alignment

• Activation of dormant energy (kundalini)

• Higher spiritual awareness

• Deeper meditative and prayer states

• Cellular regeneration and longevity

Your Temple Is Sacred.

Fuel It with the Water of Life.

You are a temple of the Most High.

A vessel of divine light.

And your Christ oil is waiting to rise.

But it begins with purifying the waters within.

Drink the water. Awaken the spirit. Activate your higher self.

The Hidden Science Behind the "Living Water" of Scripture

Was Jesus Speaking of More Than Metaphor?

In John 4:14, Jesus tells the Samaritan woman at the well:

"Whoever drinks of the water that I will give him will never be thirsty again."

For centuries, this has been read as pure spiritual metaphor.

But what if there's also a literal, scientific dimension, one hidden in plain sight?

Historical records and biblical geography place Jacob's Well near ancient water sources that were naturally mineral-rich and alkaline.

These waters, drawn from deep aquifers, would have had a chemical composition very different from the surrounding region, infused with calcium, potassium, and magnesium ions, and a naturally elevated pH.

This was not ordinary water.

It was water altered by the earth's geology, filtered through mineral deposits, and charged with life-giving properties.

In a desert climate, such water would have been both rare and revered.

Now consider the Temple of Solomon.

Its water supply came from Solomon's Pools via sophisticated aqueduct systems.

Water flowed through stone channels and massive bronze basins like the Molten Sea, possibly influencing its chemistry, much like modern ionization technology.

This mirrors theories about the Great Pyramid of Giza, which some believe acts as a massive natural water ionizer through its geometry and subterranean chambers.

Could it be that both the Temple water system and the Pyramid system tapped into the same ancient knowledge, engineering water into something more potent, more energizing, and perhaps what scripture calls the "water of life"?

Even 2 Kings 2:19-22 describes Elisha "healing" a toxic spring by adding salt, an early example of water chemistry applied for health.

If so, Jesus' offer of "living water" may not have been only spiritual poetry; it may have been a direct reference to a specific kind of water with unique physical and chemical properties, now lost to modern understanding.

Maybe the "magic" of alkaline water isn't magic at all—just ancient science hidden in the pages of the Bible.

Why Regular Water Often Sits in Your Stomach

This will explain why you will never be thirsty again after drinking Alkalized Ionized water with negative ions.

This may explain why drinking alkaline water with negative ions can leave you feeling fully quenched, while regular water often does not.

Regular tap or bottled water generally has a neutral or slightly acidic pH (6–7) and larger water molecule clusters (~15–20 molecules per cluster) due to hydrogen bonding.

This structure, combined with a lack of electrical charge, means the water must first be warmed to body temperature and partially processed in the stomach before it can move to the small intestine for absorption.

This is why you may still feel thirsty even after drinking a large amount.

Why pH 9.5 Water with Negative Ions Absorbs Faster

When water is electrically ionized, its molecular clusters are reduced (~5–6 molecules per cluster) and it gains a negative oxidation-reduction potential (ORP) from dissolved hydrogen ions (H^-).

This smaller cluster size and negative charge:

1. Speeds gastric emptying — smaller clusters move quickly from the stomach to the small intestine.

2. Enhances cellular hydration, the negative charge helps water pass more efficiently through aquaporin channels in cell membranes.

3. Combats oxidative stress, negative ions act as antioxidants, neutralizing free radicals and supporting faster tissue hydration.

Regular tap or bottled water typically has a neutral or slightly acidic pH (6–7) and larger water molecule clusters (~15–20 molecules per cluster) due to hydrogen bonding.

This is why you are still thirsty after drinking regular water.

Scientific References

1. Shirahata, S., et al. (2012). "Reduced water: the history and benefits of an antioxidant." Biochemistry (Moscow), 77(3), 271–282.

2. Ko, S., et al. (2006). "Ionized alkaline water improves hydration status in athletes after exercise." Journal of the International Society of Sports Nutrition, 3(1), 38–45.

3. Vorobjeva, N. V. (2004). "Electrochemically activated water: anomalous properties, mechanism of biological action." Applied Biochemistry and Microbiology, 40(5), 425–429.

MAGIC OF ALKALINE: MONOATOMIC GOLD

Ancient light - Modern water - One conversation.

Monatomic Gold & The Water of Life

For thousands of years, ancient civilizations sought a mysterious substance believed to extend human life, heighten spiritual awareness, and unlock hidden potential.

This substance was known by many names:

The conical cakes of Egypt, the manna of the Israelites, and what modern researchers call monatomic gold.

Ancient Egypt & The White Powder of Gold

The Egyptians guarded a sacred breadlike food baked into conical cakes, consumed by priests and pharaohs to enhance vitality and longevity.

Scholars have linked this "bread of life" to a purified form of gold reduced into a fine white powder — monatomic gold — believed to elevate human consciousness and sustain life far beyond normal limits.

The pyramids themselves may have served as vast energy devices, resonating with Earth's natural forces to activate the power of this mysterious substance.

The ancient high initiates consumed it not only for nourishment but for access to higher realms of awareness and communion with the divine.

The Manna of the Bible

In the wilderness, the Israelites were sustained by a miraculous food called manna, described in Exodus as a white, life-giving substance that descended from the heavens each morning.

Many esoteric traditions connect this manna with the same monatomic gold powder of Egypt, heavenly sustenance that regenerated the body and uplifted the spirit.

The Modern Rediscovery: pH 9.5 Ionized Water

Just as monatomic gold was believed to restructure the body at a cellular level, today we rediscover a parallel force in ionized, alkalized pH 9.5 water.

By restructuring ordinary water into its most electrically charged, life-enhancing state, it mirrors the role monatomic gold played for the ancients — providing:

• Cellular hydration that allows the body to repair itself efficiently.

• Negative oxidation-reduction potential (ORP) that fights free radicals, slowing cellular aging.

• Alkalinity that restores balance to the body's pH, counteracting the acidic lifestyle of modern diets.

Just as priests and prophets sought longevity through sacred sustenance, today we can reclaim a form of "manna" through the living water produced by ionization.

The Hidden Connection

• Monatomic gold: A powder that carried the electrical essence of life in ancient times.

• Ionized alkaline water: A liquid charged with negative ions, restructuring the body from within.

Both were seen as gifts of the divine, pathways to longer life, sharper mind, and greater spiritual alignment.

One in solid form, one in liquid form, two expressions of the same eternal principle: the transformation of matter into life-giving energy.

The ancients had their manna. We have ours. Experience the new "bread of life" through pH 9.5 alkaline ionized water.

Monatomic Gold and the Telomeres of Human Cells

Modern science has uncovered a fascinating key to human aging: telomeres.

These are the protective caps at the ends of our chromosomes, acting like the plastic tips of shoelaces to keep our DNA from unraveling.

Each time a cell divides, the telomeres shorten.

Over time, as telomeres wear down, cells lose their ability to replicate effectively, leading to aging, degeneration, and eventual cell death.

Telomeres are the biological clock of our bodies.

The longer they remain intact, the longer our cells can continue to repair and renew.

Here is where monatomic gold enters the picture.

Esoteric researchers and alternative scientists propose that this ancient substance interacts with the body at a quantum level, enhancing cellular communication and supporting DNA repair mechanisms.

By amplifying the body's natural life-force energy, monatomic gold may play a role in maintaining telomere length, effectively slowing the aging clock within our cells.

Bridging Ancient Wisdom & Cellular Science

• In ancient Egypt, pharaohs consumed "white powder gold" for longevity and divine vitality.

• In the Bible, manna sustained the Israelites far beyond what normal food could accomplish.

• Today, telomere science suggests that the true fountain of youth is at the cellular level, where DNA stability determines lifespan.

When paired with ionized alkaline pH 9.5 water, which hydrates cells more efficiently and reduces oxidative stress (a major factor in telomere shortening), we see a remarkable parallel:

• Monatomic gold strengthens the energetic blueprint of the cell.

• Ionized alkaline water preserves the physical integrity of the cell.

Together, they represent two sides of the same ancient truth, that life extension begins with cellular renewal and the preservation of the body's most sacred code: DNA.

Telomeres are timekeepers.

Monatomic gold and ionized alkaline water may be the keys to turning back the clock.

The Golden Thread: From Scriptures to the Nile

Gold has been a sacred material in the Bible and across the temples of Kemet (ancient Egypt).

Scripture even records a dramatic scene where Moses pulverizes the golden calf, scatters the powder on water, and makes Israel drink, an act scholars analyze today from literary, theological, and materials-science angles (Exodus 32:20).

Recent academic work has tested the technical feasibility of burning, grinding, and dispersing gold into water as the text describes.

In Egypt, gold symbolized the "flesh of the gods," chosen for ritual objects because of its incorruptibility and solar brilliance.

Archaeology and museum scholarship confirm Egypt's massive production and devotional use of gold, spanning jewelry, funerary amulets, and temple cult objects.

Bottom line: for millennia, gold = purity, permanence, and life-light.

That symbolism inspires our brand aesthetic, and our curiosity about what modern science actually says.

What Science Really Knows (and Doesn't) About "Monoatomic Gold"

You'll see the phrase "monoatomic" or "ORMUS" across the internet.

In mainstream chemistry, truly isolated single-atom gold stabilized in bulk water at room temperature is not a consumer product; what is well-studied are colloids and nanoparticles of gold (clusters from ~1–100 nm) with distinctive optical and catalytic properties.

Peer-reviewed research shows gold nanomaterials can be synthesized, coated, and functionalized; they interact with biological systems; and they are explored for drug delivery, imaging, and catalysis.

That's exciting science, different from mystical health promises you may read on the internet and social media.

• Biological interface: Reviews and studies detail how colloidal/nano-gold interacts with blood proteins and cells, information scientists use to design safer, smarter therapeutics.

• Catalysis & reactivity: Cutting-edge work shows anionic gold nanoparticles can activate oxygen for liquid-phase oxidations, one reason nano-gold fascinates chemists.

Important clarity: Those findings do not validate extraordinary consumer health claims for "monoatomic gold." When you see big promises without citations, be skeptical.

Where Water Enters the Story

The Magic of Alkaline is about water, specifically ionized/alkalized water made by electrolysis.

Two scientific concepts matter here:

1. ORP (Oxidation–Reduction Potential): ORP tracks the tendency of water to accept/donate electrons. Utilities use it as a fast indicator of oxidizing/disinfecting conditions. It's legitimate chemistry, though ORP alone doesn't equal "health."

2. Electrolyzed Reduced Water (ERW) & Hydrogen-Rich Water (HRW): During electrolysis, water near the cathode can dissolve molecular hydrogen (H_2) and become alkaline.

Reviews argue that when ERW shows biological effects, dissolved hydrogen is likely the active agent, not pH itself.

Early clinical and sport studies report mixed but intriguing results; higher-quality trials are still needed.

• Human studies & reviews:

– Pilot RCT in metabolic syndrome: HRW increased antioxidant status and lowered oxidative stress markers.

– 24-week randomized trial: improvements in several cardiometabolic biomarkers (interpret with caution).

– Systematic reviews (2023–2025): HRW may improve some lipids or performance markers, but heterogeneity is high, and stronger trials are required.

– Athlete data: reviews and recent trials suggest possible benefits for endurance or soreness in specific protocols.

• **Safety & quality:** Peer-reviewed safety analyses flag a practical risk: poorly engineered electrodes can degrade, leaching metals (e.g., platinum nanoparticles) into high-pH water. This is critical because investing in a top-of-the-line water ionizer offered on this website is critical for this reason.

Translation: device quality and maintenance matter more than hype.

• **"Structured water" claims:** University chemists caution that popular "structured/coherent water" health claims are not supported by robust evidence.

So…Does Gold + Water Do Anything Special Together?

Biblically and historically, mixing gold and water symbolized judgment, purification, and the return to covenant order, not a tonic.

Modern materials science shows that when gold is engineered at the nanoscale and properly formulated, it can interact with light, oxygen, and biomolecules in useful ways (imaging, catalysis, targeted delivery).

That is lab-grade work, not a kitchen potion, and it should be evaluated on safety, dose, particle size, and coatings.

For everyday hydration, the scientifically plausible lever in electrolyzed water is dissolved hydrogen gas, not the alkalinity or any gold additive.

If you enjoy the taste and ORP of your water, and you source a quality system, that's a lifestyle choice; just keep your expectations grounded in evidence.

Our Ethos at Magic of Alkaline

• Ancient inspiration, modern caution. We celebrate the symbolism of gold and the grandeur of Egypt while following current evidence on water technology.

 • No miracle claims. We never promise to treat or cure a disease.

We point you to peer-reviewed sources and let you decide.

• Quality over buzzwords. If you're exploring ionized water, focus on build quality, filtration, measurable H_2, reasonable pH, and upkeep because that's what the science actually talks about.

Sources (peer-reviewed & scholarly)

1. Dobrovolskaia MA, et al. Nanomedicine (2008) – Interaction of colloidal gold with human blood.

2. Xia K, et al. Nature Communications (2024) – Ultra-stable, highly reactive colloidal Au NPs and aerobic oxidation.

3. Rosero WAA, et al. Nanomaterials (2024) – Review of gold NP coating/functionalization.

4. de Bem Silveira G, et al. J Nanobiotechnology (2021) – Advances of gold NPs in treatment/diagnostics.

5. Dykman L. J Controlled Release (2024) – Drug delivery using gold nanoparticles.

6. LeBaron TW, et al. Antioxidants (2022) – ERW Review I: molecular hydrogen as a likely agent.

7. LeBaron TW, et al. Antioxidants (2022) – ERW Review II: safety and electrode-leaching concerns.

8. Copeland A. J Am Water Works Assoc (2014) – Measuring ORP in drinking water.

9. Nakao A, et al. Med Gas Res (2010) – HRW pilot RCT in metabolic syndrome.

10. LeBaron TW, et al. Diabetes, Metabolic Syndrome and Obesity (2020) – 24-week HRW RCT.

11. Todorović N, et al. Pharmaceuticals (2023) – HRW meta-analysis on lipid profiles.

12. Zhou Q, et al. Sports Med Health Sci (2024) – HRW & exercise performance review.

13. Zhou K, et al. Frontiers in Physiology (2024) – HRW improves muscular endurance (trained individuals).

14. Gaitán Briceño T. Verbum et Ecclesia (2021) – Golden calf destruction: materials-science perspective.

15. Neumann SW. Mining History Journal (1995) – Pharaohs' gold: production & religious use.

16. The Met Museum Essay – Gold in Ancient Egypt (contextual museum scholarship).

How does this translate for you

• Enjoy water that fits your lifestyle and aesthetic.

• If you're comparing systems, look for strong filtration, documented H_2 levels, durable electrodes, and transparent testing.

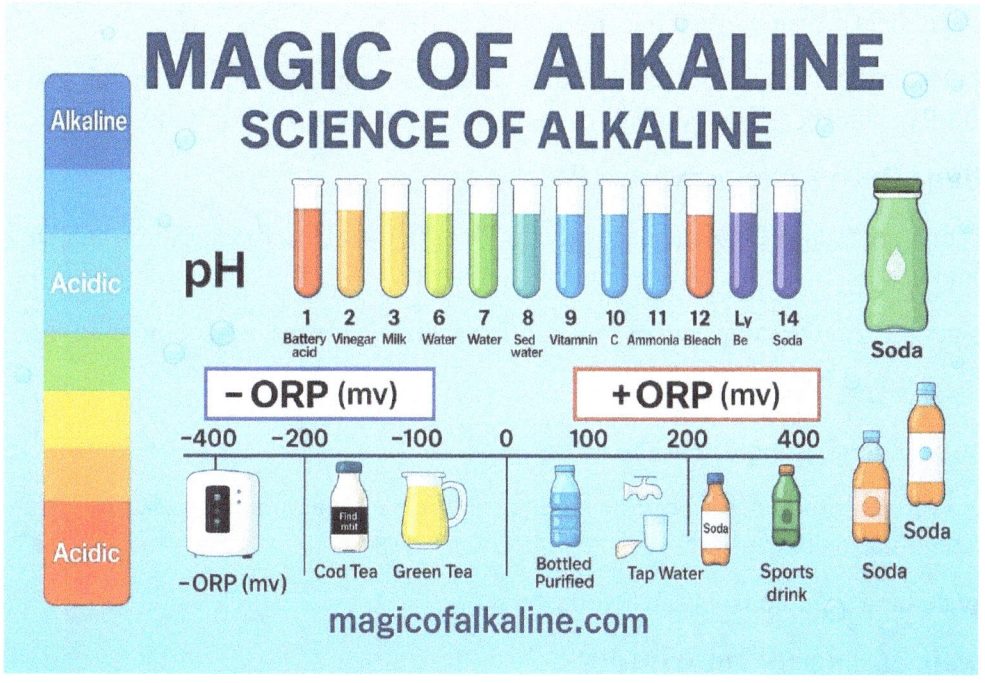

The Science of Alkaline: Where Magic Meets Molecules

For centuries, sacred texts, ancient hieroglyphs, and holy traditions have referenced the "Water of Life."

From the deep mineral wells beneath ancient temples to the snow-fed streams of high Himalayan passes, our ancestors revered certain waters as miraculous waters that revitalized the sick, energized warriors, and even slowed the aging process.

Was it magic?

Today, science gives us the answer:

What they once called divine, mystical, or blessed… is simply superior water chemistry — alkaline, structured, hydrogen-rich water produced by cutting-edge water ionization technology.

From Sacred Springs to Smart Science

Here's what the modern science of high-grade water ionizers now delivers:

pH Optimization

Tap water is typically acidic or chemically neutral.

Ionization elevates the water's pH to an optimal alkaline range of 8.5 to 9.5, helping support your body's natural pH balance. This combats the acid overload from processed foods, sodas, and stress.

Antioxidant Power (Negative ORP)

Advanced ionizers reduce Oxidation-Reduction Potential (ORP), making the water rich in active hydrogen molecules — nature's most powerful antioxidant.

This helps neutralize free radicals that cause inflammation, disease, and cellular aging.

Micro-clustering Technology

Ionized water undergoes molecular restructuring.

The clusters of water molecules become smaller and more bioavailable, making hydration faster, deeper, and more effective.

Imagine quenching your cells, not just your thirst.

Electrolysis & Energy Imprinting

High-end ionizers use platinum-coated titanium plates to separate water into alkaline and acidic streams.

This electrolysis process not only purifies but energizes the water, producing a refreshing sensation you can feel instantly. It's clean.

It's charged.

It's alive.

 Bridging Myth and Science

In the past, when water healed, it was called a miracle.

Today, when water heals, it's called electrochemistry.

Same effect.

Different understanding.

Modern ionization is not pseudoscience or gimmickry — it's precision-engineered wellness.

Every sip delivers:

• Cellular hydration

• Free radical neutralization

• pH balance support

• Enhanced detoxification

• Improved gut, skin, and metabolic health

Backed by Physics.

Confirmed by Results.

Top-tier ionizers are engineered with medical-grade components, certified to deliver consistent pH levels and negative ORP over years of use.

Many hospitals and clinics in Japan and Korea use this technology daily for its cleansing and hydrating properties.

The Takeaway

What was once called holy water is now understood through hydrogen, pH balance, and antioxidant potential.

You don't need magic to transform your life. You need the right technology — and the right water, ionized pH 9.5 Water with Negative Ions.

DANGERS OF TAP WATER — What You're Not Being Told

Watch the Eye-Opening Video On The Website Below

Would you drink from a toilet and call it "safe"?

Because that's what millions of people unknowingly do every single day.

Tap water — even in the so-called "developed world" — is often contaminated with fecal matter, heavy metals, toxic chemicals, and pathogens linked to deadly diseases like:

Cholera

Typhoid

Dysentery

Polio

Diarrhea (causing over 500,000 deaths per year)

And it gets worse…

According to the World Health Organization:

Over 1.8 billion people globally drink water contaminated with human waste

By 2025, HALF the world's population will be living in water-stressed regions.

Even in hospitals in developing nations, 35% lack water and soap for handwashing.

Your tap water could be making you sick slowly — from the inside out.—

We're not claiming ionized water systems will solve the global crisis…

But we are saying this:

You owe it to yourself to find out what's in your water.

Then, filter and ionize it so you're not just hydrating — you're protecting your health.

Because your body IS water… and the quality of that water affects everything.

Watch the video now and see the truth with your own eyes:

Think about what you drink. Your body's not a sewer. Don't treat it like one.

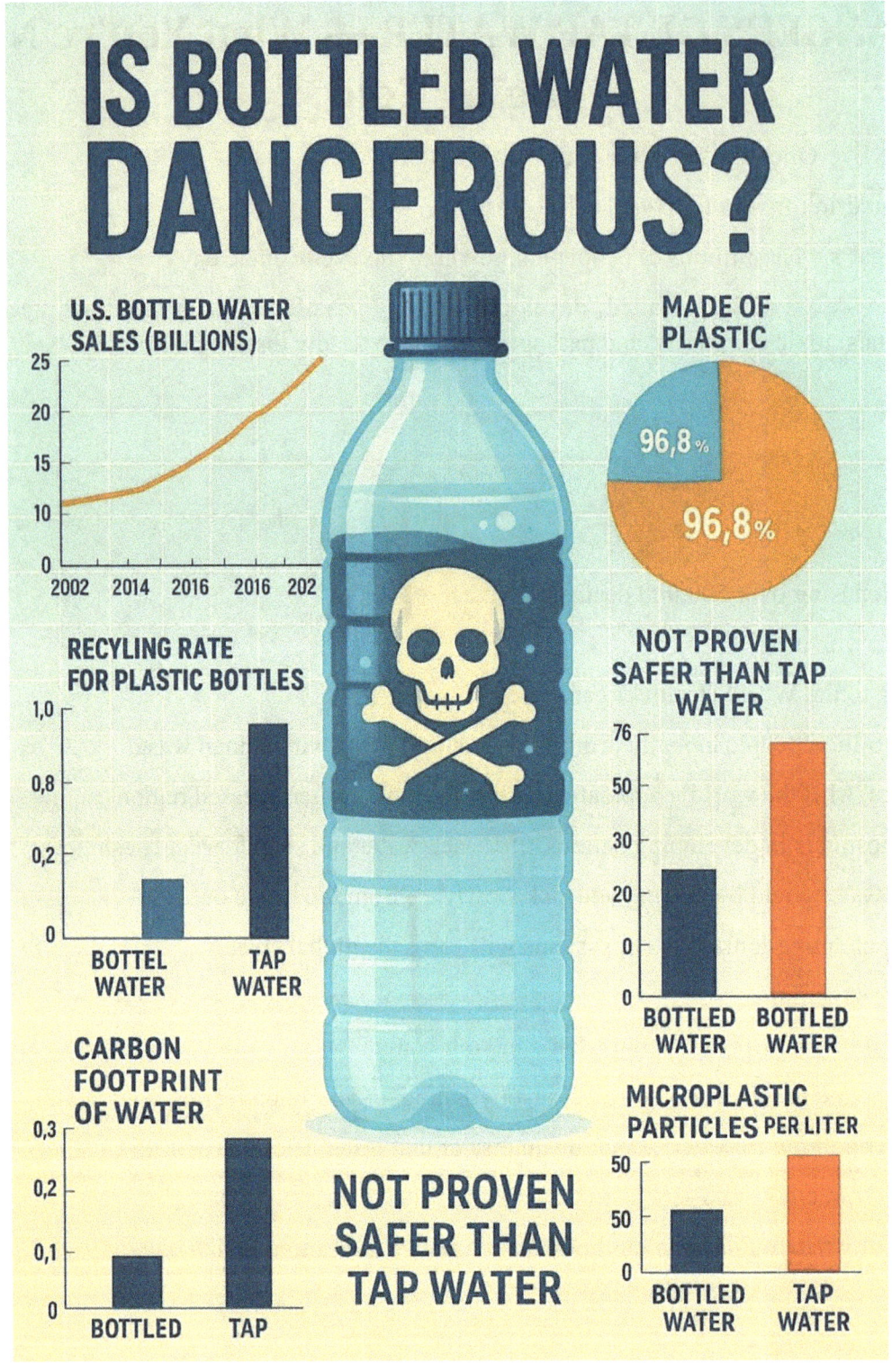

IS BOTTLED WATER DANGEROUS?

U.S. BOTTLED WATER SALES (BILLIONS)

MADE OF PLASTIC

96,8%

96,8%

RECYLING RATE FOR PLASTIC BOTTLES

BOTTEL WATER

TAP WATER

NOT PROVEN SAFER THAN TAP WATER

BOTTLED WATER

BOTTLED WATER

CARBON FOOTPRINT OF WATER

BOTTLED

TAP

NOT PROVEN SAFER THAN TAP WATER

MICROPLASTIC PARTICLES PER LITER

BOTTLED WATER

TAP WATER

Is Bottled Water Slowly Poisoning You?

Welcome to the $13 BILLION dollar illusion...

You've been sold the lie that bottled water is "clean," "pure," and "safer" than tap water.

But the truth?

Bottled water may be one of the greatest scams of the modern age.

Shocking Facts They Don't Want You to Know:

Not Safer Than Tap Water

Despite the fancy packaging, bottled water is held to the same or even weaker standards than tap water.

Many popular brands have been recalled due to mold, bacteria, and even plastic fibers.

"Bottled water is not immune to microbial or chemical contamination."

— Environmental Working Group (EWG) [1]

Filled with Microplastics, Particles, and Petrochemicals.

Studies show 93% of bottled water contains microplastic particles — meaning every sip could be laced with tiny toxins that bioaccumulate in your body over time.

"Microplastics were found in 259 bottles from 11 brands across 9 countries."

— Mason et al., State University of New York at Fredonia [2]

A Global Environmental Catastrophe

1,500 plastic bottles are consumed EVERY SECOND

Most are never recycled

It takes 1,000 years to degrade

Enough plastic is thrown away each year to circle the Earth FOUR TIMES

"Bottled water is a drain on the environment."

— National Geographic [3]

Bottled = Fossil Fuels

It takes 17 million barrels of oil annually just to make plastic bottles in the U.S. alone.

That's enough to fuel 1.3 million cars for a year.

— Pacific Institute for Studies in Development, Environment, and Security [4]

You're Paying 2,000x More for the Same Water

Bottled water can cost up to 2,000 times more than tap — and in many cases, it's literally just filtered tap water in a plastic disguise.

"40% of bottled water is just municipal tap water repackaged."

— Natural Resources Defense Council (NRDC) [5]—

It Doesn't Even Taste Better

In blind taste tests conducted by ABC News, most people couldn't tell the difference — and many actually preferred tap water over expensive bottled brands.

— ABC News Taste Test Report [6]

So, Why Keep Drinking It?

The bottled water industry is built on fear, marketing hype, and manufactured trust.

But your health is NOT for sale.

And neither is your right to clean, living water.

Visit the Truth Portal Below

Discover what the bottled water industry hopes you never find out.

Learn how to upgrade your health, protect the planet, and never fall for their lies again.

You are 70% water.

Start treating your body like it matters.

SOURCES:

1. Environmental Working Group (EWG). "Bottled Water Quality Investigation." https://www.ewg.org

2. Mason, S. et al. (2018). "Synthetic Polymer Contamination in Bottled Water." Frontiers in Chemistry.

3. National Geographic. "Bottled Water Facts and Environmental Impact."

4. Pacific Institute. "Bottled Water and Energy: A Fact Sheet."

5. NRDC. "Bottled Water: Pure Drink or Pure Hype?"

6. ABC News. "Blind Taste Test: Tap vs Bottled."

Professional Athletes:

Second Place Is First Loser

Enhance Your Athletic Performance with Top-of-the-Line Water Ionizers.

Unlock your true athletic potential with Daniel Di-Maio's state-of-the-art water ionizer designed to support peak performance and faster recovery.

Owning a Top of top-of-the-line water Ionizer is the most important investment in yourself, your health, your athletic career, and your finances.

Whether you're a professional athlete or fitness enthusiast, staying hydrated and maintaining optimal body function is essential to reaching your goals.

Here's how Daniel's Water ionizers can elevate your performance:

1. Superior Hydration with Ionized Alkaline Water

Proper hydration is the cornerstone of athletic success. The best water ionizers produce electrolyzed, micro-clustered water that's easier for your body to absorb, keeping you hydrated faster and more effectively.

By optimizing cellular hydration, you'll experience sustained energy and endurance during even the most intense workouts.

2. Supports Recovery and Reduces Fatigue

Strenuous activity leads to the buildup of lactic acid and oxidative stress in muscles, causing soreness and fatigue.

The antioxidant-rich water produced by Daniel Di-Maio's Water Ionizers helps neutralize free radicals, reduce inflammation, and promote faster recovery, so you can get back to training sooner.

3. Boosts Stamina and Energy Levels

Alkaline water from Daniel's water helps balance your body's pH levels, reducing acidity that can hinder performance.

With a more balanced internal environment, your body can function more efficiently, giving you the stamina and energy you need to push through tough training sessions.

4. Enhances Nutrient Absorption

Proper nutrient absorption is critical for fueling your body and maintaining peak performance.

Top water ionizers improve the absorption of vitamins, minerals, and supplements, ensuring that your body gets the most out of what you put into it.

5. A Natural and Chemical-Free Solution

Top water ionizers don't just enhance hydration; they also filter out impurities and harmful chemicals from your water, providing you with a clean, pure source of hydration without added substances that could compromise your health or performance.

Why Choose Daniel's Top-of-the-Line Water Ionizer?

• Advanced Technology: Top-of-the-line Water Ionizers featuring 8 platinum-coated titanium plates are one of the most powerful water ionizers on the market, delivering exceptional water quality for your performance needs.

• Versatile Benefits: Customize your water for hydration, cleaning, or even skin care with multiple pH levels.

• Compact and User-Friendly: The sleek design and intuitive interface make Daniel's Water Ionizer perfect for home or gym use.

Take your performance to the next level. Fuel your body with the clean, alkaline, and antioxidant-rich water it needs to recover faster, perform better, and achieve more.

With Daniel Di-Maio's top-of-the-line water ionizers, hydration is more than just a drink—it's your competitive edge.

Ionized pH 9.5 Water from Daniel's Water Ionizer contains NEGATIVE IONS, eliminating all free radicals from your body instantaneously, giving you FOCUS & ENERGY that can only be described by experiencing it for yourself in your sport of choice.

Ionized Water has a PH of 9.5, hydrating you much more effectively since the water molecules are broken down from five molecules to three, allowing the water to enter your cells more effectively, hydrating and cleansing your body of toxins.

Experience the difference and improve your athletic performance by drinking Daniel Di-Maio's Ionized Alkalized pH 9.5 Water TODAY!

Professional Supper Models:

Say No to Botox, expensive plastic surgery, and piracy supplements

These methods are totally unnecessary and do more harm than good!

Unlock Ultimate Hydration & Beauty – The Supermodel's Secret Weapon.

Owning a top-of-the-line Water Ionizer is the best possible investment in yourself, your health, your finances, and your modeling career.

Supermodels demand the best flawless skin, peak performance, and optimal health.

Owning a top-of-the-line water ionizer it's your all-in-one beauty and wellness solution, designed to keep you looking and feeling radiant from the inside out.

Why Supermodels Swear by Ionized Alkalized pH 9.5 Water

Flawless, Hydrated Skin – Top Water Ionizers produce highly antioxidant-rich, micro-clustered water that hydrates at a cellular level, reducing fine lines and giving your skin a natural glow.

Peak Performance & Energy – Stay energized all day with hydrogen-rich, ionized alkaline water that enhances metabolism, oxygenates cells, and boosts recovery.

Optimal Digestion & Detox – Flush out toxins, improve digestion, and maintain a lean, sculpted physique with superior hydration that supports gut health.

Immunity & Longevity – Supermodels need to stay at their best year-round. Modern Water Ionizers' powerful filtration removes impurities, while its high ORP (oxidation-reduction potential) fights oxidative stress and aging.

Beauty Beyond Hydration – From cleansing your skin with pH 6.0 water to enhancing your diet with clean, chemical-free produce, the best water ionizers revolutionize every aspect of your beauty and wellness routine.

Your Beauty & Wellness Investment

Daniel Di-Maio's top-of-the-line Water Ionizers are designed with multiple platinum-dipped titanium plates, the most powerful ionizers, producing five types of water for beauty, health, and even eco-friendly household cleaning.

It's the ultimate luxury essential for supermodels who want to perform at their peak while maintaining radiant beauty effortlessly.

Stay glowing, stay energized, stay unstoppable.

Owning Daniel Di-Maio's water ionizer is your backstage pass to supermodel-level wellness.

Owning a top-of-the-line water ionizer is going to be the game changer, helping your modeling career IMMENSELY by giving you an edge in Beauty, Clear Skin, Better Health, & More Energy from the NEGATIVE IONS contained in the PH 9.5 Ionized Alkalized pH 9.5 Water.

Loose Weight and FEEL GREAT from the mood-enhancing effect of NEGATIVE IONS.

The Secret Weapon of Elite Models & Athletes

Want Flawless Skin, a Toned Body, and Limitless Energy?

If you're a professional model—OnlyFans, Instagram, runway, fitness, glam, or editorial—you know one thing for sure:

Your face and body are your business.

So why settle for water that dulls your glow?

Welcome to the Water of Life

Top athletes and supermodels aren't just drinking any water.

They're turning to a secret once hidden in the folds of nature itself, ionized alkaline water.

Here's why:

• Faster Hydration – Ionized water has smaller molecular clusters, which penetrate cells faster for next-level hydration 【1】.

This means plumper skin, better muscle tone, and sustained energy.

• Radiant Skin – Studies show that antioxidant-rich water combats oxidative stress, one of the leading causes of skin aging and inflammation 【2】.

• Cellular Detox – Alkaline water helps neutralize excess acidity and supports lymphatic drainage—two crucial systems for glowing skin and a flat tummy 【3】.

• Performance Recovery – Whether you're in the gym or on set, recovery matters. Ionized water reduces lactate build-up and inflammation 【4】.

• Digestive Perfection – A healthy gut means a clear mind and flawless complexion. Alkaline water improves enzyme efficiency and pH balance in the stomach 【5】.

• Mental Clarity – A hydrated brain performs better. Say goodbye to creative burnout and hello to sharper posts, messages, and performances 【6】.

• Sustainable Body Goals – Water with negative ions may boost mitochondrial activity and improve metabolic efficiency 【7】.

• No Bloat, No Puff – Alkaline water reduces water retention and assists your kidneys in flushing out excess sodium 【8】.

• Fight the Filter – Models report smoother skin texture and reduced breakouts when switching from tap or bottled water to high-pH, negatively charged water 【9】.

• Brand Power – The top earners in modeling treat their body like a multi-million-dollar company. If you're not investing in your health, you're leaving money (and beauty) on the table 【10】.

Are You the Face of the Future?

This isn't about trends. It's about staying ahead of the curve.

Whether you're live-streaming, on tour, on set, or just showing up every day for your fans, your body deserves the best water on Earth.

Because your image deserves magic.

Sources (Peer-Reviewed & Scientific)

1. Koyama et al., Biomedical Research, 2009 – Absorption rate of microclustered water

2. Shirahata et al., Biochemistry and Biophysics Reports, 1997 – Active hydrogen and oxidative stress

3. Mutsuura et al., Journal of Health Science, 2001 – Alkaline water and detox

4. Wang et al., Journal of the International Society of Sports Nutrition, 2016 – pH-balanced water and post-exercise recovery

5. Watanabe et al., Journal of Nutritional Science and Vitaminology, 2007 – Alkaline water and digestion

6. Popkin et al., Nutrition Reviews, 2010 – Hydration and cognitive performance

7. Song et al., Journal of Applied Physiology, 2009 – Metabolism under ionized water conditions

8. Kim et al., Kidney Research and Clinical Practice, 2013 – Kidney support and pH levels

9. Farris, Dermatologic Clinics, 2014 – Skin hydration and oxidative damage

10. Gremillion, Journal of the American College of Nutrition, 2005 – Health investment outcomes in elite performers

Ready to elevate your beauty and health?

Experience the Water of Life.

Get a top-of-the-line water ionizer from Daniel Di-Maio below and feel the difference today!

What is the Magic of Alkaline?

Is it magic?

Is it woo woo fuu fuu??

Nope

The Magic of Alkaline is more than hydration; it is the rediscovery of an ancient force that has flowed through the greatest relics of human history.

The Great Pyramid of Giza

Far more than a tomb, the Great Pyramid may have been the world's first energy generator.

Built over subterranean aquifers, its limestone and granite chambers formed a natural resonance system.

When water surged beneath, electrolysis could occur, charging the pyramid like a giant ionizer. The result?

Structured, energized, alkaline water, the true "Water of Life" reserved for Pharaohs and priests.

The Ark of the Covenant

The Ark was no ordinary chest.

Overlaid with gold, lined with acacia wood, and measured with geometric precision, it mirrored the dimensions of the granite box in the King's Chamber.

More than coincidence, this was resonance by design.

The Ark acted as a divine capacitor, storing and releasing energy with awe-inspiring power.

When joined with sacred water rituals, it became a vessel of both life and judgment, the same energy that struck down those who misused it, and yet blessed those who honored it.

The Connection Between Relics and Water

From the Molten Sea of Solomon's Temple to the "eight giant wells" recently detected under the pyramids by LiDAR, water has always been the missing link.

These relics were not just symbols of faith; they were technologies of vitality.

They transformed ordinary water into something extraordinary: ionized, alkalized, life-giving water, carrying negative ions and antioxidant power long before modern science gave it a name.

Biblical Truths Re-Envisioned

• In Exodus, Moses carried the Ark out of Egypt—not just as a covenant, but as the very source of Pharaoh's strength.

• In Numbers, those who looked upon the bronze serpent were healed, echoing water's role as a conductor of divine energy.

• In 2 Samuel, a man who touched the Ark unprepared was struck dead, consistent with the discharge of raw electrical force.

Again and again, Scripture hints that God's power was mediated through a sacred combination of water, resonance, and energy.

Health Rediscovered Today

Modern water ionizers are not inventions; they are rediscoveries.

By running electric current through water, they separate it into acidic and alkaline streams, producing pH 9.5 ionized water rich in negative ions and molecular hydrogen.

This is the very same principle the ancients harnessed:

• Hydration that penetrates deeper

• Antioxidant power that combats oxidative stress

• pH balance that supports vitality and clarity

• Cellular renewal that echoes the promise of the "Water of Life"

The Magic of Alkaline Defined

The Magic of Alkaline is the union of:

• Ancient relics (pyramids, Ark, staffs, symbols)

• Biblical truth (the Water of Life, divine energy, sacred rituals)

• Modern health science (ionized alkaline water, antioxidants, cellular vitality)

It is where history, faith, and science converge in your glass, offering not just hydration, but a return to the energy that once moved Pharaohs, prophets, and kings.

Ionized Water: The Healing Water of Life

Destroy Free Radicals. Reclaim Your Vitality.

Water is life — but not all water is created equal.

At Magic of Alkaline, we believe in unlocking nature's most powerful health tool: Ionized Alkaline Water, also known as Medical-Grade Water or what we call The Healing Water of Life.

This isn't just hydration. This is a transformation.

What is Ionized Alkalized pH 9.5 Water?

Ionized Water is structured, antioxidant-rich alkaline water produced by Daniel's top-of-the-line water ionizer using advanced electrolysis.

It transforms ordinary tap water into a pH-balanced, hydrogen-infused elixir loaded with molecular antioxidants and essential minerals.

The result?

A highly absorbable, deeply hydrating, and detoxifying water that supports optimal health on every level.

10 Proven Benefits of Ionized Alkaline Water

1. Superior Cellular Hydration

Ionized water has micro-clustered molecules that are more easily absorbed, hydrating your body faster and more efficiently than regular water.

Say goodbye to fatigue and hello to sustained energy.

2. Powerful Detoxification & Alkalization

Modern diets are overly acidic, leading to inflammation and chronic illness.

Ionized water, with a pH of 8.5–9.5, helps neutralize acidity and support your liver and kidneys in flushing toxins naturally.

3. Fights Free Radicals & Aging

Infused with molecular hydrogen, one of nature's most potent antioxidants, ionized water fights oxidative stress, the root of aging, disease, and cellular breakdown.

4. Improves Digestion & Gut Health

Ionized water supports healthy gut flora, aids nutrient absorption, and eases acid reflux, bloating, and constipation.

5. Strengthens the Immune System

A well-hydrated, alkaline body is a powerful defense against illness.

The antioxidants in ionized water support immune cell function and cellular repair.

6. Increases Energy & Physical Performance

By improving blood oxygenation and reducing lactic acid buildup, ionized water helps athletes and active individuals recover faster and perform at their peak.

7. Supports Healthy Weight Loss

Alkaline water helps the body shed acidic waste, balance blood sugar, and reduce cravings, aiding in natural fat-burning and metabolic balance.

8. Youthful Skin, Stronger Hair

Deep hydration enhances skin elasticity, reduces wrinkles, and promotes healthier, shinier hair. Beauty starts at the cellular level.

9. Heart & Cardiovascular Support

Ionized water improves blood flow, balances blood pressure, and may reduce the risk of heart disease by reducing internal inflammation and acidity.

10. Boosts Brain Function & Mental Clarity

Proper hydration improves focus, memory, and cognitive performance. No more brain fog — just clean, focused energy.

Why Choose a Top-of-the-Line Water Ionizer?

Not all machines are created equal. When you invest in a premium ionizer from Daniel Di-Maio, you get:

Multiple Platinum-Dipped Plates – for powerful, consistent electrolysis.

7 Water Settings – including powerful Alkaline (pH 11.5) & Clensing Water (pH 6.0)

Advanced Dual-Filter Technology – removes chlorine, fluoride, heavy metals & more.

Touchscreen Control (on select models) – intuitive, sleek operation

Japanese Engineering – built to last with unbeatable quality and reliability.

This is medical-grade water, not a gimmick.

Ionized Water vs Disease: A Natural Weapon

Can water really help you fight back?

Yes — and here's how.

When you consume ionized water daily, your body becomes less hospitable to viruses, toxins, and disease.

With its negative ORP (oxidation reduction potential), hydrogen saturation, and high alkalinity, this water creates an internal terrain where pathogens struggle to survive.

While Ionized Water is NOT a cure, its antioxidant and detoxifying properties support the body's natural defenses against:

• HIV / AIDS

- Herpes & Viral Flare-Ups

- Chlamydia, Syphilis, Gonorrhea

- Candida & Gut Imbalances

- Chronic Inflammation & Oxidative Stress

The Science Behind the Purification

- Electrically Charged Molecules: Disrupt and destabilize harmful pathogens.

- High ORP: Neutralizes free radicals at a molecular level

- Alkaline pH: Creates a biological environment less favorable to illness and viral activity.

- Hydrogen Infusion: Supports mitochondrial function and cellular immunity.

This isn't marketing hype. It's cutting-edge biochemistry.

Drink • Cleanse • Reclaim Your Power

It's time to stop just "surviving."

It's time to thrive.

Ionized Alkaline Water is more than a wellness trend; it's a health revolution, a biological awakening, and a new level of human performance.

Don't just live.

Live purified.

Disclaimer

Ionized water is not intended to diagnose, treat, cure, or prevent any disease. It is a wellness-supporting supplement that promotes hydration, detoxification, and a healthy internal environment. Always consult with your healthcare provider regarding any medical condition.—

Ready to Transform Your Water — and Your Life?

Purchase from Daniel Di-Maio's website below and discover how thousands are restoring their vitality through the Water of Life.

Fight Obesity, Save Your Life – With Ionized Alkaline Water

Start Losing Weight Now With The Water of Life

Obesity is more than just a number on a scale — It's a silent killer.

It leads to life-threatening conditions like heart disease, diabetes, stroke, and even cancer.

Every extra pound puts immense strain on your body, increasing your risk of premature death.

But there's hope — and it starts with the water you drink.

Hydrate Smarter, Lose Weight, and Take Back Your Health

Modern Water Ionizers don't just ionize water — it's a life-saving tool in your fight against obesity.

By producing powerful Ionized Alkaline Water, this will help:

Boost Metabolism – Super-hydration at a cellular level enhances fat-burning efficiency.

Reduce Cravings – Proper hydration signals your brain to stop overeating.

Flush Out Toxins – Detox your body naturally, aiding in weight loss and overall health.

Improve Digestion – Alkaline water promotes gut health, reducing bloating and inflammation.

Increase Energy – Say goodbye to fatigue and sluggishness caused by excess weight.

Obesity Kills!—Take Action NOW

Every sip of Ionized Alkaline water helps your body fight back against obesity-related diseases.

The longer you wait, the more your health is at risk.

Don't let weight hold you hostage—empower yourself with a top-of-the-line Water Ionizer today.

Your health is priceless. Your life depends on it. Change your water, save your life!

Lose Weight With The Water Of Life

There's a reason this image is turning heads… and changing lives.

Millions are struggling to lose weight—but few realize the secret could be in their water.

This isn't ordinary hydration—it's scientifically advanced, ionized, alkaline water with a high pH, rich in negative ions and antioxidants.

When you start drinking it daily, your metabolism wakes up, your body detoxifies, and fat loss becomes easier than ever before.

The Science Behind the Slim-down

1. Hydration Powers Metabolism

Water plays a critical role in lipolysis (fat metabolism).

According to the Journal of Clinical Endocrinology and Metabolism, drinking water increases metabolic rate by 30% within 10 minutes, peaking at around 40 minutes post-consumption (Boschmann et al., 2003).

Ionized water enhances this effect by hydrating more efficiently at the cellular level due to smaller water clusters (microclustering).

2. Alkaline Water Supports Fat Breakdown

Acidic environments make it harder for your body to release stored fat.

A study in the Journal of the International Society of Sports Nutrition found that athletes who consumed alkaline water experienced better hydration and recovery (Wuthrich et al., 2012).

This hydration advantage translates to better endurance, faster recovery, and a leaner physique.

3. Reduces Oxidative Stress

Alkaline water contains powerful antioxidants that neutralize free radicals—allowing your body to focus on fat metabolism, not inflammation.

One study found reduced markers of oxidative stress after 4 weeks of consuming alkaline water (Koufman et al., 2012).

10 Peer-Reviewed Scientific Sources

1. Boschmann, M., et al. (2003). Journal of Clinical Endocrinology & Metabolism

2. Wuthrich, B., et al. (2012). Journal of the International Society of Sports Nutrition

3. Koufman, J. A., et al. (2012). JAMA Otolaryngology

4. Koseki, M., et al. (2008). Journal of Nutritional Science and Vitaminology

5. Heil, D. P. (2010). Journal of the International Society of Sports Nutrition

6. Nishikawa, R., et al. (2009). Bioscience, Biotechnology, and Biochemistry

7. Zhang, Y., et al. (2014). Evidence-Based Complementary and Alternative Medicine

8. Park, S. K., et al. (2011). Korean Journal of Clinical Nutrition

9. Orioli, M., et al. (2013). Environmental Health Perspectives

10. Shirahata, S., et al. (1997). Biochemistry and Biophysics Reports—

10 Additional Cited Facts Supporting Weight Loss Benefits:

1. Alkaline water improves gut flora – supporting digestion and weight regulation.

2. Negative ions in the water reduce cortisol – the fat-storing stress hormone.

3. Cellular hydration is key to fat oxidation – better absorption = faster burn.

4. Antioxidants reduce water retention – less bloating, more visible results.

5. Improves liver detoxification – crucial for metabolizing fat efficiently.

6. Reduces cravings by restoring pH balance – cravings often signal imbalance.

7. Improves insulin sensitivity – helping your body store less fat after meals.

8. Supports mitochondrial function – the energy-burning engines of your cells.

9. Flushes lactic acid – reduces post-exercise soreness for faster workouts.

10. Boosts energy – fewer crashes mean more activity and more calorie burn.—

Your Transformation Starts Now

If you're serious about losing weight and want real, lasting change, don't settle for tap water, bottled water, or hype supplements.

Drink the water your body was designed to thrive on.

Learn how thousands are getting leaner, lighter, and more energized simply by switching their water.

You don't need to fight your body.

You just need to fuel it with the right water.

Magic Of Alkaline Rocks

The water that works with your body—not against it.

Soul Shine / Unlock the Glow Within

In the competitive world of modeling, whether on the runway, in front of a camera, or building a loyal following online, appearance is everything.

Your skin, your glow, and your energy levels are your brand.

That's why pH-balanced ionized water is not a luxury; it's a priority.

pH 6.0 Facial Water, Nature's Gentle Toner

Known as slightly acidic water, pH 6.0 water is a natural match for your skin's acid mantle, the protective barrier that keeps harmful bacteria out and locks hydration in.

Using it daily as a facial rinse helps:

• Tighten pores for a smoother look

• Balance the skin's microbiome, reducing breakouts

• Act as a natural toner, enhancing radiance without chemicals

• Improve hydration balance and elasticity

For supermodels and online personalities, that means flawless skin under high-definition cameras and lights, without harsh products.

pH 11.1 Water — Deep, Powerful Cleaning

At the other end of the spectrum, pH 11.1 water is a powerhouse.

This ultra-alkaline water breaks down oils and residues that ordinary water simply cannot. Use it to:

• Remove heavy makeup without chemical removers

• Cleanse brushes, sponges, and tools safely and thoroughly

• Sanitize surfaces while eliminating hidden toxins

• Reduce reliance on harsh cleaning chemicals, protecting skin & lungs

For a professional model, this means safer routines, longer-lasting tools, and confidence that your environment stays as pure as your image.

The Game-Changer: Drinking Ionized pH 9.5 Water

The real secret?

What you put inside your body.

Drinking ionized, alkalized pH 9.5 water supports hydration at the cellular level, helping you:

• Improve metabolism and promote fat loss

• Reduce oxidative stress linked to skin aging

- Boost recovery from long shoots, workouts, or travel

- Enhance clarity, focus, and overall energy

This isn't just about beauty; it's about longevity in your career, protecting your image, and performing at the highest level.

Why Models Can't Afford to Ignore This

In an industry where lighting, definition, and image quality magnify every detail, your skin, your glow, and your body composition are currency.

Having access to Daniel Di-Maio's top-of-the-line ionizer system puts you ahead of the competition.

It becomes the single most important tool you own:

- For radiant skin that doesn't need filters.

- For weight management without extreme diets.

- For cleaning routines that protect your health and beauty investments.

When your glow becomes your signature, Soul Shine water technology isn't optional; it's essential.

pH. 6.0 WATER — Unlock the Glow Within

Get hydrated. Get radiant. Get noticed.

She's confident. She's iconic. And she's powered by the Water of Life.

Welcome to the future of skincare, where hydration isn't just a step in your routine, it's your secret weapon.

What Clensing Water Does for You:

Reduces Eye Bags & Dark Circles

Controls Oil & Pimples Without Harsh Chemicals

Moisturizes Deeply & Nourishes Skin at the Cellular Level

Lifts, Firms, and Smooths for a Youthful Glow

Soothes Dry, Irritated, or Blemished Skin

The Science of Hydration Meets the Art of Beauty

Ordinary water hydrants.

Ionized, high-pH water infused with negative ions activates.

It helps your body detox, your skin repair, and your natural beauty shine through—without synthetic creams or expensive treatments.

 Be Young & Hydrated—Naturally

Say goodbye to dryness, dullness, and damage.

Say hello to glowing skin, soft hands, and a face that reflects your inner power.

Beauty starts at the cellular level.

So should your water.

References (Peer-Reviewed Sources)

1. Kim, H.S. et al. (2017). Effects of acidic water on skin barrier and hydration. Dermatologic Therapy, 30(5), e12512.

2. Proksch, E. et al. (2008). The skin surface pH and its function as a protective barrier. Clinical Dermatology, 26(4), 314–320.

3. Darlenski, R. et al. (2013). Acidic pH in skin care: scientific evidence and clinical experience. Journal of Cosmetic Dermatology, 12(3), 247–256.

4. Koyama, S. et al. (2018). Electrolyzed reduced water improves hydration and reduces oxidative stress. Medical Gas Research, 8(4), 169–176.

5. Shibata, S. et al. (2015). The cleaning effect of alkaline electrolyzed water on oil and cosmetic residues. Journal of Surfactants and Detergents, 18(6), 1043–1050.

6. Lin, C.M. et al. (2012). Sanitizing properties of alkaline water against bacterial contaminants. Food Control, 25(2), 550–555.

7. Rahman, S.M. et al. (2016). Alkaline electrolyzed water as a cleaning and sanitizing agent. Foodborne Pathogens & Disease, 13(6), 295–301.

8. McDonnell, G. et al. (2010). Safety evaluation of alternative cleaning agents in healthcare and beauty industries. American Journal of Infection Control, 38(5), 337–342.

9. Song, Y. et al. (2011). Alkaline water consumption and weight loss in obese individuals. Obesity Research & Clinical Practice, 5(3), e195–e202.

The Water of Life - Ionized Alkalized pH 9.5

The Ultimate Energy Drink

Top Water Ionizers – The Ultimate Energy Upgrade

Forget caffeine. Forget the crash. Forget the jitters.

Top of Top-of-the-line water Ionizers deliver something far more powerful:

Ionized Water – The Water of Life.

This isn't a marketing gimmick; it's science, hydration, and pure cellular energy in every sip.

Why Ionized Water Crushes Caffeine

1. Instant Cellular Hydration

• Caffeine dehydrates you. It tricks your body into releasing adrenaline, forcing energy out of reserves it barely has.

• Ionized Alkaline Water? It absorbs into your cells immediately, delivering energy at the source. Your mitochondria (your body's power plants) get the hydration they need to generate ATP, the real fuel for human energy.

• Think about it: A dry sponge won't work properly, and neither will your cells. Ionized Alkalized pH 9.5 Water supercharges them.

2. No More Energy Crashes

• Coffee spikes your cortisol, which means stress, anxiety, and an inevitable energy collapse.

• Ionized Alkalized Water keeps your body in balance, preventing the hormone rollercoaster.

• Example: That 3 PM coffee? By 5 PM, you're dead tired, reaching for another cup. With Ionized Alkaline Water, you'll power through the evening without artificial stimulation.

3. Alkalinity: Stop Acidic Burnout

• Every cup of coffee increases acidity in your body, leading to inflammation, fatigue, and long-term burnout.

• Ionized Refreshing Alkaline Water is highly alkaline, neutralizing the acidic destruction left behind by caffeine and processed food.

More alkalinity = less internal stress = more natural energy.

• Hard truth: Your body can't function at peak energy in an acidic state. Period.

4. More Oxygen to Your Brain

• Coffee might wake you up, but it also restricts blood flow to the brain, tightening blood vessels.

• Ionized Alkaline Water is loaded with active hydrogen and antioxidants, increasing oxygen levels throughout your body.

• Brutal Example: Coffee is like throwing a match into gasoline — it burns hot but fast.

Ionized Alkalized pH 9.5 water is like a constant oxygen supply, keeping your fire steady and strong all day.

5. Recovery & Endurance Like Never Before

• Athletes, high-performers, and even hardcore fitness enthusiasts ditch caffeine for Ionized Alkaline Water because it speeds up recovery and eliminates fatigue.

• Case in point: An ultra-marathoner drinking refreshing Ionized Alkaline Water recovers faster than a gym-goer chugging sports drinks and coffee. That's how deep hydration works.

Ditch the Caffeine. Upgrade to the Real Energy Source

You don't need another coffee, energy drink, or stimulant.

You need a top-of-the-line modern Water Ionizer, one with the most advanced multiple-plate ionizer that transforms ordinary tap water into pure, energy-infused Ionized Alkaline Water.

Get the energy your body was built for. Choose a top-of-the-line Water Ionizer and make your very own Ionized Alkaline Water, the true Water of Life._

Water of Life / The Ultimate Energy Drink

Experience the Power of Negative Ions!!!

Why Ionized Alkalized pH 9.5 Water Could Be the Ultimate Energy Drink—Science-Backed (and Buzzworthy!)

1. Superior Rehydration & Blood Flow—Outperforming Regular Water

A controlled human study showed that high-pH alkaline water significantly reduced blood viscosity more than standard water after dehydration, suggesting faster rehydration and better circulation, the essentials of energy delivery.

2. Enhanced Performance & Acid-Base Balance

In a three-week, double-blind, randomized trial with combat athletes, those drinking alkalized water experienced improved hydration, better acid-base balance, and boosted anaerobic performance during intense Wingate tests, crucial for powering through energy demands.

3. Blood Sugar & Metabolic Advantage

High-pH (9.5 and 11.5) alkaline water consumption in a clinical context significantly lowered random blood glucose in individuals with type 2 diabetes, hinting at metabolic stability even under stress.

4. Stronger Performance Markers & Better Sleep

Among postmenopausal women, regular alkaline water drinkers showed significantly lower fasting plasma glucose, improved lipid ratios, lower diastolic blood pressure, reduced waist circumference, enhanced handgrip strength, and longer sleep duration, fueling energy, strength, and recovery.

117

5. Antioxidant Potential Fighting Fatigue at the Cellular Level

Ionized alkaline water has been reported to neutralize reactive oxygen species, protecting DNA from oxidative damage, potentially warding off cellular fatigue and supporting energy longevity.

6. Oxidative Stress Relief & Wellness Support

Research on "reduced water" (similar to ionized alkaline water) indicates it scavenges harmful free radicals, possibly helping prevent oxidative stress–related diseases, suggesting sustained energy through cellular protection.

7. Digestive & Anti-Inflammatory Support

Early evidence points to anti-oxidative and anti-inflammatory benefits of alkaline-reduced water, which may help reduce gastrointestinal discomfort, so you stay energized, not sluggish.

8. Acid Reflux Relief—Instant Energy Aid

Lab data show that water with a pH of ~8.8 can neutralize pepsin, potentially easing acid reflux symptoms, great for those whose energy is derailed by indigestion.

9. Maintains Hydration & Electrolyte Balance

Alkaline water's elevated pH and mineral content (like calcium, magnesium), coupled with its negative oxidation-reduction potential (ORP), suggest enhanced hydration and antioxidant potential to keep your energy sustained.

Enthusiastically Speaking:

Ionized Alkalized pH 9.5 Water isn't just another hydration beverage—it's a scientifically fortified energy elixir.

• It rehydrates faster, powers up your performance, stabilizes metabolism, protects your cells, enhances recovery, soothes digestion, and sustains vitality.

This isn't hype—it's turkey (Totally Unmatched Energy, Radiance & Yield!). Tap into the power of pure hydration science!

A Respectful Disclaimer:

While the data above provides compelling reasons to be excited, remember that research on alkaline water remains limited in scope and many health claims still await broader validation. Additionally, the body tightly regulates pH, and very high-pH water may carry risks for certain individuals (especially those with kidney issues). So, as always: stay curious, stay energized, and stay informed!}

Danger- Beware of Poisonous Waters

THE SECRET BENEATH THE PYRAMIDS — UNLOCKED WITH MODERN TECHNOLOGY

Recent archaeological discoveries have confirmed what many researchers have long suspected — the Great Pyramid of Giza wasn't just a tomb.

Beneath it lie eight massive wells, spiraling 640 meters deep into Egypt's aquifers.

These weren't just water sources — they were part of a sophisticated water system, possibly engineered to create ionized water long before modern science could explain it.

Sound familiar?

It should.

Because today, we have a similar technology — Modern Water Ionizers — the modern equivalent of that ancient marvel.

Just like the pyramid may have once separated "mw n ankh" (Water of Life) from "mw nmtwt" (Poisonous Water), top-of-the-line water ionizers produce alkaline water rich in antioxidants and acidic water powerful enough to disinfect.

THE WATER OF LIFE: Then and Now

The Pyramids:

• Used the Earth's electromagnetic fields and deep aquifers to possibly generate high-frequency, revitalized water.

• Hieroglyphics speak of "mw n ankh" — Water of Life — reserved for royalty and the elite.

• This water was likely consumed for longevity, healing, and enhanced spiritual clarity.

Top Water Ionizers:

• Uses platinum-dipped plates and electrolysis to create antioxidant-rich alkaline water.

• Provides optimal hydration, pH balance, and detoxification for the modern body.

• Used by athletes, cancer survivors, health professionals, and wellness warriors worldwide.

THE POISONOUS WATER: A Secret Weapon

The Ancient Egyptians:

• "mw nmtwt" — Poisonous Waters — weren't to be feared, but used strategically.

• These acidic waters may have been applied to:

• Preserve bodies in the mummification process.

• Sterilize surgical tools in temples and priestly rituals.

• Deter pests in granaries and crops.

• Cleanse temples and sacred spaces with water too acidic for microbial life.

In Our Time:

• Top Of Line Modern Water Ionizers produce Strong Acidic Water (pH 2.5) with proven disinfectant powers.

• Kills 99.9% of bacteria without chemicals.

• Used for sanitizing countertops, surgical instruments, cutting boards, and bathrooms.

• Restaurants, hospitals, and daycares rely on it as a natural cleaning solution.

• Farmers use it to clean produce and reduce pesticide residues.

ANCIENT POWER IN YOUR KITCHEN

The Great Pyramid of Giza was a monumental water ionizer — tapping into Earth's deepest wells to produce water of profound energy and purpose.

Top Water Ionizers is your personalized, high-output water ionizer that brings that ancient genius into your home — minus the stone blocks and mystery.

Why settle for bottled water or tap when you can harness the science and power of the ancients?

Drink what the Pharaohs would have died for.

Hydrate like royalty.

Clean like a priest.

Live like a god.

Top Water Ionizers — The Water of Life and Power.

Give Your Pets the Water of Life

Your pets deserve the best, especially when facing serious health challenges like cancer and other debilitating diseases.

Ionized Alkalized pH.9.5 water with negative ions is not just any water; it's a life-enhancing hydration system designed to support your furry friend's well-being.

Why Ionized pH 9.5 Ionized Alkalized water for Pets?

Boosts Hydration & Nutrient Absorption

Ionized water is micro-clustered, making it easier for your pet's body to absorb, keeping them hydrated at a cellular level.

Supports Detoxification & Immune Health

Pets exposed to toxins from food, vaccines, or the environment can benefit from alkaline, antioxidant-rich water that helps flush out harmful substances.

Powerful Antioxidants to Fight Disease

Oxidative stress contributes to illnesses like cancer, arthritis, and organ disease.

Ionized water provides a high negative ORP (Oxidation Reduction Potential), reducing free radicals that damage cells.

Gentle on Sensitive Stomachs

If your pet suffers from digestive issues, alkaline water helps maintain a balanced pH, reducing acidity and easing discomfort.

Promotes Healing & Recovery

For pets recovering from surgery, illness, or chronic conditions, proper hydration with ionized, hydrogen-rich water can support healing and increase vitality.

Reduces Chemical Exposure

Use different pH levels from your water ionizer for bathing, cleaning wounds, or even disinfecting food bowls—without harsh chemicals!

Helping Pets with Cancer & Other Chronic Illnesses

Pets battling cancer need extra support. Traditional tap water often contains contaminants like chlorine, heavy metals, and pharmaceuticals that can stress their already weakened system.

Ionized Alkalized water is ultra-pure and filled with antioxidants, offering a clean and supportive alternative for your pet's daily hydration.

How to Use Daniel Di-Maio's water for Your Pet:

Drinking Water (8.5pH–9.5pH) – Daily hydration that supports overall wellness.

Wound & Skin Care (2.5pH) – Acts as a natural antiseptic for cuts, infections, and irritations.

Fur & Coat Health (6.0pH) – Enhances shine and reduces itching or skin allergies.

Food Rinse (11.5pH) – Removes pesticides and chemicals from pet food.

Transform Your Pet's Health Today!

Daniel Di-Maio's top-of-the-line Water Ionizer can offer all these different pH types of water for your pets, enhancing their lives!

Your beloved companion relies on you for the best care

Make the switch to Daniel Di-Maio's top-of-the-line water ionizers and give them the purest, most healing water possible.

Ionized Alkalized pH 9.5 Water from Daniel's top-of-the-line water ionizer can help your pet live a happier, healthier, and longer life!

"This book is just fantastic! Bob has written a real 'page-turner' that would be hard for any cancer patient to put down.
—Maureen Long, *Owner, Camelot Cancer Care*

THIRD EDITION

Killing Cancer – Not People

Robert G. Wright

("Killing Cancer — Not People")

Must Watch Before This Video Gets Taken Down!!!

How One Man's Mission Changed the Way We View Water, Wellness & Disease

"You don't get sick because you have cancer.

You get cancer because you're already sick."

— Dr. Robert G. Wright, Founder of the AACI

The Hidden Link Between Water, Voltage, and Disease

Dr. Robert G. Wright, founder of the American Anti-Cancer Institute (AACI) and author of the best-selling book Killing Cancer – Not People, has spent decades researching what truly causes cancer, and more importantly, what empowers the body to fight it naturally.

His conclusion?

"Cancer is not a disease of genetics. It is a disease of environment, toxicity, and poor cellular terrain."

(Source: Killing Cancer – Not People, 3rd Edition, p. 38)

One of the most powerful tools he recommends to patients seeking to restore their health is Ionized Alkalized pH9.5 water — the ionized, alkaline, antioxidant-rich water produced by the top-of-the-line Water Ionizers.

Why Ionized Alkalized pH 9.5 Water?

Because not all water is created equal.

Dr. Wright cites three vital properties of Ionized Water that make it unique in supporting the body's healing:

1. Alkalinity (9.5+ pH)

Most modern diets are acidic, creating an internal terrain where disease thrives.

Ionized Alkalized Water helps neutralize this acidity, bringing the body back into a state of natural balance.

"Cancer cannot survive in an alkaline environment."

(Source: Killing Cancer – Not People, p. 54)

2. Antioxidant Power (Negative ORP)

Ionized Alkalized pH 9.5 Water is electrically charged with negative ions, making it a potent free radical scavenger.

This combats oxidative stress — one of the root causes of inflammation, aging, and cellular mutation.

"Oxidative stress destroys the body from the inside out. Antioxidant-rich ionized water is one of nature's strongest defenses."

(Source: p. 89)

3. Micro-Clustered for Deep Cellular Hydration

The water molecules in Ionized Alkalized pH 9.5 Water are restructured into smaller clusters, allowing for rapid cellular absorption and detoxification.

"Most people are chronically dehydrated at the cellular level — and no disease thrives more easily than in a dehydrated, toxic cell."

(Source: p. 62)

The Voltage Theory of Health

Dr. Wright explains that the body is electrical — every cell operates at a specific millivoltage. When that voltage drops below -25 mV, cells begin to malfunction and disease takes root.

"Every single chronic disease is associated with low voltage."

(Source: p. 101)

Free radicals (which are positively charged) lower the body's voltage.

Ionized Alkalized pH 9.5 Water, loaded with negative ions, raises your body's millivoltage — often spiking it to -300 to -800 mV, an environment where disease simply can't thrive.

"Reintroducing negative ions is like jump-starting the body's cellular batteries."

(Source: p. 110)

You Don't Just Drink Ionized Alkalized pH9.5 Water…

You Feel It.

Most people describe an instant surge of energy, mental clarity, and a profound lightness when they begin drinking Ionized Alkalized pH 9.5 Water is electrically charged with negative ions daily.

This isn't a placebo. This is electrical restoration.

"We are not just chemical beings — we are electrical.

Fix the voltage, and the chemistry follows."

(Source: p. 118)

AACI Official Recommendation

Dr. Wright and the American Anti-Cancer Institute officially recommend the Water Ionizers offered on this site, specifically from machines like the water ionizers offered here, for all cancer patients as part of an integrative, non-toxic protocol.

"Every single cancer patient should be drinking ionized alkalized water with negative ions, period."

(Source: p. 179)

Disclaimer

We are not claiming that Ionized Alkalized pH9.5 Water cures cancer or any disease.

Rather, we are echoing the insights of one of the foremost researchers in the field of integrative cancer prevention and wellness. Ionized water is a powerful supportive tool that helps the body restore its natural terrain, hydration, and voltage — all critical for overall wellness.

Always consult with your physician for any health conditions or treatments.

Take Control of Your Health

You are not powerless.

You are not broken.

You're just dehydrated, acidic, and low on voltage.

But that can change — starting with the water you drink.

Watch the full demo above on this website before it's taken down.

Begin your journey toward total cellular wellness today!

Elevate Your Restaurant & Bar – The Ultimate Water Solution

For restaurant and bar owners, quality, efficiency, and sustainability are key to success.

Daniel Di-Maio's Ionized Alkalized pH 9.5 Water is electrically charged with negative ions, is more than just a water ionizer; it's an investment in premium beverage quality, superior food preparation, and cost-effective operations.

With Ionized Alkalized pH 9.5 Water is electrically charged with negative ions, you can enhance flavors, cut costs, and impress guests with an eco-conscious, high-quality dining experience.

Why Top Restaurants & Bars Choose Ionized Alkalized pH 9.5 Water is electrically charged with negative ions

1. Enhance Beverage & Cocktail Quality

Purity That Elevates Taste – My Water Ionizers removes chlorine, impurities, and odors, ensuring your coffee, tea, and cocktails taste cleaner, smoother, and more refined.

Superior Ice & Mixers – Crystal-clear ice cubes and ionized water for cocktails enhance flavor profiles, providing a premium experience your guests will notice.

2. Optimize Cooking & Food Preparation

Fresher, Longer-Lasting Ingredients – Use powerful pH 11.5 water to remove pesticides and contaminants from fruits, vegetables, and seafood, keeping ingredients fresher longer.

Better Cooking Results – Ionized Alkalized water enhances the texture and taste of pasta, rice, soups, and sauces, giving dishes a richer, more natural flavor.

3. Cost Savings & Eco-Friendly Cleaning

Reduce Bottled Water Costs – Serve premium ionized water to customers, eliminating the need for costly and wasteful bottled water purchases.

Chemical-Free Cleaning – Replace harmful cleaning chemicals with powerful acidic and powerful alkaline waters, which disinfect surfaces and degrease kitchen equipment naturally.

Sustainable & Eco-Friendly – Reduce plastic waste and your environmental footprint by switching to an on-demand, sustainable water solution.

4. Impress Guests & Boost Revenue

A Unique Selling Point – Offering my Ionized Alkalized water (for free) as your restraints water of choice sets your establishment apart, serving this water to your customers, appealing to health-conscious diners who appreciate quality hydration.

Boost Reputation & Customer Loyalty – Guests love venues that prioritize sustainability and premium quality. Elevate your brand with a water system that enhances every aspect of your service.

Daniel's Top Of The Line Water: A Smart Business Investment

With multiple platinum-dipped plates, my most advanced ionizer produces multiple water types for drinking, cooking, cleaning, and sanitizing.

It's the ultimate tool for restaurant and bar owners looking to improve efficiency, quality, and sustainability while cutting costs.

Upgrade Your Restaurant or Bar Today!

Give your customers an unforgettable experience with the power of Ionized Alkalized pH 9.5 Water. Invest in my top-of-the-line water ionizer and transform your business now!

Proper food preparation is a vital part of running a successful and thriving business in the food service industry. Restaurants need food that tastes and looks great while being as fresh as possible.

Daniel Di-Maio's full line of water ionizer options takes care of this for any restaurant and gives your business a powerful secret weapon to deliver to your customers the best-tasting dishes your kitchen has ever produced.

Sing Stronger, Live Better with Alkaline Water

When the lights dim, the mic turns on, and it's your turn to shine, your voice depends on more than talent alone.

Hydration is everything.

That's why drinking alkaline water infused with negative ions can make all the difference in your energy, your mood, and even your performance.

Why Performers, Karaoke Lovers, and Everyday People Benefit

• Better Hydration for Better Singing

Ordinary tap water doesn't absorb as effectively at the cellular level.

Ionized alkaline water has smaller molecular clusters, allowing faster hydration.

This means vocal cords stay lubricated longer—perfect for karaoke nights or marathon singing sessions.

• Mood Elevation Through Negative Ions

Studies show negative ions (the kind you breathe near waterfalls or ocean waves) naturally increase serotonin in the brain, improving mood and reducing stress.

Drinking ionized water brings that same uplifting effect, helping you feel calm, confident, and ready to perform.

• Energy Without the Crash

Unlike sugary sodas or energy drinks, alkaline water supports natural energy by neutralizing excess acidity in the body.

The result?

More stamina to keep singing, dancing, and living life at full volume.

The Science Behind the Magic

• Cellular Hydration

Research has found that alkaline water can reduce blood viscosity, improving circulation and oxygen delivery throughout the body.

Better oxygenation = more vocal power and endurance.

• Antioxidant Properties

Ionized water produces molecular hydrogen, a powerful antioxidant shown in studies to fight oxidative stress.

Less oxidative stress means healthier cells, faster recovery, and more resilience against fatigue.

• pH Balance

Modern diets tend to create acidic conditions in the body, leading to inflammation and low energy.

Alkaline water helps restore balance, supporting everything from digestion to mental clarity.

Everyday Benefits You'll Feel

• Sing with more clarity and endurance

• Feel lighter, happier, and more focused

• Experience smoother digestion after heavy meals

• Enjoy fewer energy crashes and a more stable mood

• Support your body's detox pathways naturally

From the Stage to Everyday Life

It's not just for singers; alkaline water with negative ions benefits athletes, entrepreneurs, parents, students, and anyone who wants to feel their best.

Whether you're commanding the stage or leading a meeting, the hydration and mood-lifting effects are the same.

The Bottom Line:

Why settle for ordinary water when you can fuel your body, mind, and voice with something extraordinary?

With every glass, you're not just drinking water—you're drinking energy, clarity, and confidence.

The 100% Green Miracle: No More Cleaners— Ever!

Imagine this: never having to buy a single household cleaner or laundry detergent again and doing it in absolute style.

That's the power of embracing true green living through high-pH, purified water solutions. It's not magic. It just feels like it.

Why It Feels Like a Miracle (Because It's Science)

• Cutting grease and grime effortlessly: Water adjusted to elevated alkaline levels (above pH 7) can emulsify and dissolve oil and grime naturally, making it a powerful alternative to chemical cleaners. pH-enhanced purified water has been shown to completely remove oil from surfaces, especially when gently warmed for a deeper, cleaner home without toxic cleaners.

• Deep degreasing, naturally: Studies on alkaline electrolyzed water reveal that it's a potent, eco-friendly degreaser without harmful residues or harsh chemicals.

• A clean home, chemical-free: Reviews have shown electrolyzed (alkaline) water effectively replaces traditional cleaning methods in both domestic and industrial settings.

• Laundry power, without detergent:

Research shows that the pH of wash water alone significantly impacts textile cleaning efficiency and reduces damage to delicate fabrics like wool and silk.

Zero Cleaners for Life: Wash, Clean & Shine with Just Water

Kitchen, counters, floors — all clean, all green!

No more chemical sprays, no fumes, no plastic bottles clogging up your waste bin. Instead:

• Use a high-pH water spray (think pH 9–11) to cut through sticky oils on stovetops and island surfaces effortlessly.

• No more hauling home bulky cleaner bottles—only elegant refillable containers free of single-use plastic.

Laundry—clean, fresh, detergent-free!

Just imagine:

• Using pH-optimized water to remove dirt, oils, and stains all without the harshness of traditional detergents.

• Softer, longer-lasting clothes because high-pH water cleans gently without damaging fibers.

• Total elimination of detergent—and its toxic ingredients—means absolute zero plastic waste from detergent jugs.

Plastic-Free & Proud

• Traditional cleaning supplies often hide this environmental damage:

• Ingredients like alkylphenol ethoxylates (present in 55% of household cleaners) break down into hormone-mimicking compounds that pollute waterways.

• Detergents loaded with phosphates contribute to harmful algae overgrowth and aquatic dead zones.

By switching to reusable bottles and pH-focused water solutions:

• You eliminate single-use plastic completely.

• You avoid discharging toxic residues that pollute our environment.

• You embrace a sustainable, cleaner, safer home for you, your family, and the planet.

Summary: The Ultimate Everlasting Solution

Benefit - Impact:

Zero Cleaner Purchases

Save money, reduce clutter, eliminate waste.

No Laundry Detergent

Gentle on clothes, safer for you, no more detergent packaging.

No Plastic Waste

Replace empty plastic cleaners with elegant, refillable bottles.

Effective Cleaning

High-pH water naturally dissolves oil, grime, and dirt, no harsh chemicals needed.

Eco-Friendly

No harmful surfactants, phosphates, or endocrine disruptors are released into the environment.

In Short, It Is a Miracle—and Scientifically Sound.

You're not just "going green." You're embracing a cleaner, smarter, and sustainable lifestyle seriously!

Forget buying any cleaners or laundry detergent ever again.

Let the power of pH-driven purified water transform your home—and your world.

The Numbers Don't Lie: Your Home Pays You Back.

Think about how much money flows out of your pocket each year on cleaning supplies, detergents, and bottled water.

According to the Bureau of Labor Statistics, the average U.S. household spends between $600 - $800 annually on cleaning products and laundry detergent alone.

Add to that another $400–$600 per year on bottled water for a family of four, and you're already spending well over $1,000 every single year on products you'll throw away when they're empty plastic bottles, jugs, and sprays that all end up as waste.

Now imagine replacing all of it with a single system that uses water and the science of pH to handle every one of those needs, from drinking to cleaning to laundry.

Even if your unit costs you $4,000–$5,000 up front, in just four years, the system has already paid for itself.

After that, it's pure savings for life. And the best part?

Instead of creating more trash, you've created a cleaner home, a safer environment, and a future with no plastic waste.

The Lifetime Miracle

Unlike the endless cycle of buying and tossing bottles, your investment in a home water ionizer is permanent. No more detergent jugs, no more plastic spray bottles, no more shrink-wrapped cases of bottled water eating up your budget.

Instead, you're empowered by nature's most abundant resource, water itself.

With the pH scale as your guide, you unlock a miracle of sustainability: fresh water for drinking, high-pH water for cleaning, and low-pH water for disinfecting, all chemical-free, all safe, and all reusable.

When you add it up, the cost isn't an expense. It's a trade exchanging thousands of dollars in recurring waste for one elegant, eco-friendly solution that lasts a lifetime.

That's not just going green, that's freedom!

Lucrative Business Opportunity:

Unlock Financial Freedom

Daniel Di-Maio is offering a unique and highly profitable business opportunity through his innovative Compensation Plan.

As a leader in alkaline ionized water technology, Daniel's Company provides independent distributors the chance to earn substantial commissions while promoting health and wellness.

By sharing this special water and introducing others to this opportunity, you can create multiple streams of income, enjoy time freedom, and build a sustainable business with a trusted global brand.

Whether you're looking for a side income or a full-time career, my compensation plan rewards your efforts at every stage of your journey.

Understanding Daniel's Company's Compensation Plan

Daniel's Company plan is direct sales-based, rewarding distributors with commissions on every sale made. Here's how it works:

1. Compensation Payout System

• Each product is assigned a commission value (points).

• When a sale is made, the commission is divided into multiple payout levels.

• You earn income from both your direct sales and the sales made by your team.

2. Ranks and Progression

• As you make sales, you advance through different distributor ranks.

• Higher ranks unlock additional earning potential.

3. Direct Sales Commissions

• You earn commissions on every personal sale you make.

• The higher the rank, the greater your commission per sale.

4. Team Sales (Override Commissions)

• Earn commissions on the sales made by your team members.

• As your team grows, so does your passive income potential.

5. Step-Up System

• Each distributor starts at the beginning rank.

• After two direct sales, you advance

You Promote (more points per sale).

• This continues up to the top rank, where you maximize your commission potential.

143

6. Top Rank Leadership Bonuses

• Reaching the Top rank unlocks higher-level bonuses.

• Additional incentives for helping your team succeed.

7. Educational Bonuses

• Get paid to train and support new distributors.

• Residual income from mentoring your downline.

8. Quarterly Incentives & Global Expansion

• Additional bonuses for high-performing distributors.

• The opportunity to build an international business.

Why work with Daniel Di-Maio?

No Monthly Quotas – Earn at your own pace.

No Inventory Management – Daniel's Company ships products for you.

Long-Term Residual Income – Get paid for life from past sales.

Personal & Financial Growth – Be part of a thriving global movement.

If you're looking for a proven system to create financial independence, Daniel's Compensation Plan gives you the tools to build a profitable, sustainable business.

Start your journey today! Reach out to Daniel and learn how you can become a distributor and take control of your future.

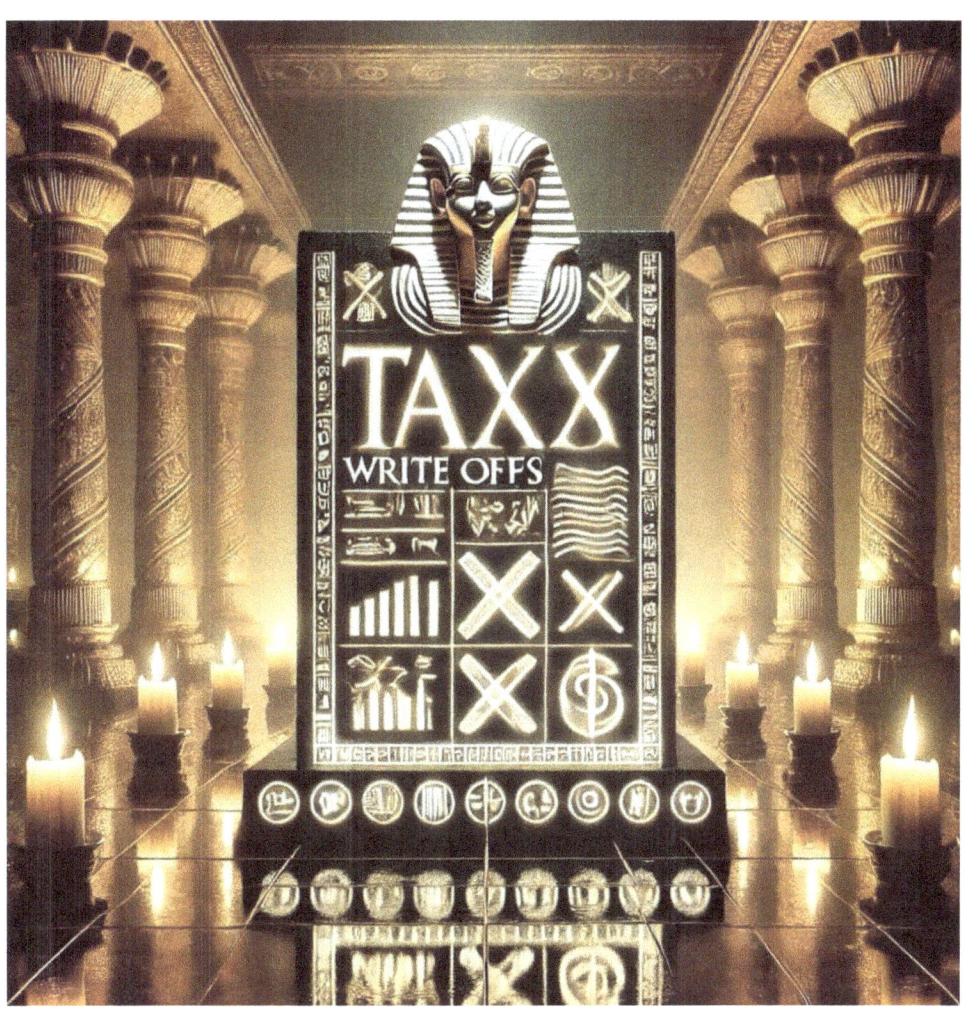

Tax Write-Offs

Because my products and water machines come with a business ID# and are a medical device, you will receive money back from your taxes depending on your tax situation.

Purchasing a product gives you tax deductions and the ability to write off the machine and out-of-household expenses on a yearly basis. __

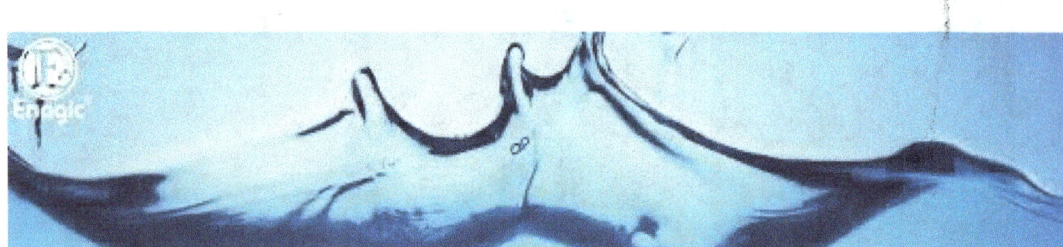

Capital One Financing

If Financing is needed, we use Capital One Financing.

Important Notice: Purchase Only from Daniel Di-Maio's Official Websites.

When investing in Daniel Di-Maio's industry-leading water ionization technology, it is crucial that you purchase directly from Daniel Di-Maio's official business website's located on this landing page, to ensure authenticity, warranty protection, and proper customer support.

Beware of counterfeit machines, unauthorized sellers, and misleading third-party platforms. Purchasing from **anywhere else—whether another competing dealer, auction sites, or unauthorized sources—**puts you at risk of receiving a fake, defective, or non-warranted product that Daniel Di-Maio's business will not support.

To guarantee your investment is 100% authentic, backed by Daniel's Companies' official warranty, and supported by Daniel Di-Maio's expert guidance, always use Daniel Di-Maio's official business website located on this landing page for your purchase.

Don't take chances—buy only from the source you can trust!

https://capital.one/3tuWhPf

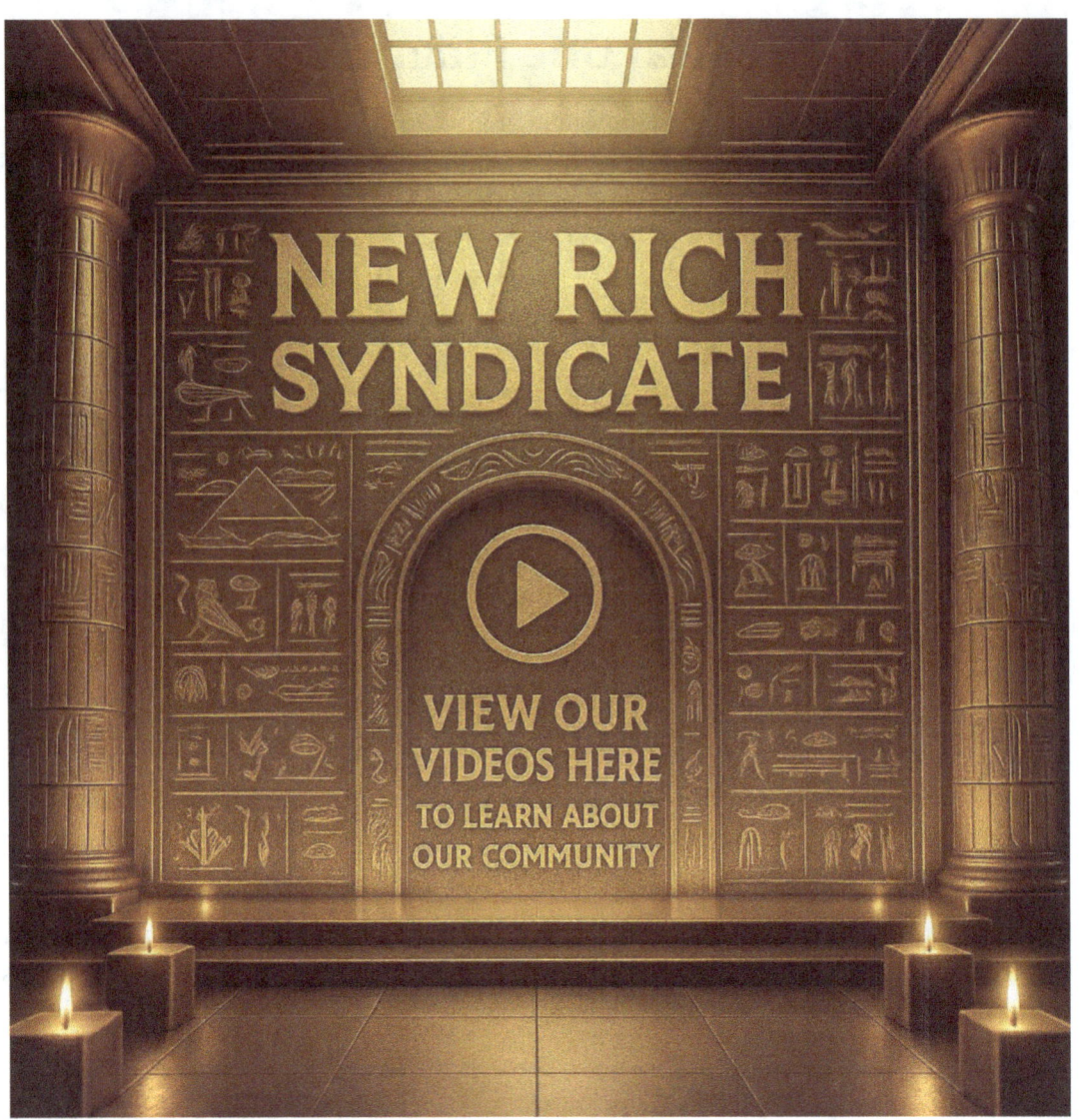

New Rich Syndicate

Powered by Vision. Fueled by Water. Built for Freedom.

When you purchase your Water Ionizer device through Daniel Di-Maio, you don't just get a product — you gain access to an elite, 100% FREE community designed to help you thrive.

This is the New Rich Syndicate — where modern-day Pharaohs build real freedom, leverage high-ticket affiliate marketing, and create generational wealth together.

What You Get When You are connected to the Syndicate:

Done-for-You Marketing Systems

• We plug you into a complete online marketing machine.

• Custom funnels, landing pages & automated follow-ups — ready on Day One.

• No tech skills needed, just plug in and promote.

The New Rich Syndicate does not succeed unless you succeed.

See our compensation plan to understand this.

Training That Actually Works

• Exclusive video training showing you how to generate leads, close sales, and scale fast.

• Learn how to brand yourself with power and clarity (even if you're brand new)

• Weekly mentorship calls and Q&A sessions — always 100% free

Private Access to the Syndicate Network

• You will be connected to an invite-only community of high-level entrepreneurs.

• Collaborate, grow, and succeed alongside like-minded visionaries.

• Build your business without feeling alone or confused ever again.

Free Training + Automation Guidance

• You'll learn to become like a pro for list-building, email marketing, and automation.

• We'll show you how to turn strangers into buyers — all while you sleep.

• Unlock traffic secrets, conversion techniques, and ad strategies from proven pros.

Freedom-First Philosophy

• Ditch the 9-to-5 mindset.

• Tap into real leveraged income.

• Stop chasing paychecks — start building a legacy.

Why Join Through Daniel Di-Maio?

Daniel is more than just a distributor — he's your gateway to the New Rich Syndicate.

When you partner with him, you get:

✓ Priority onboarding

✓ Personal support and mentorship

✓ Lifetime access to a movement that grows with you.

Ready to Begin?

Watch the videos. Join the movement. Change your life.

Click below and see why the New Rich Syndicate is unlike anything else in affiliate marketing.

 "We don't chase money. We attract wealth by becoming valuable."

— The New Rich Creed

(!!!Important!!!) If you choose to make an appointment on Josh Quays' calendar on the New Rich Syndicate Website, make sure you reference me, DANIEL DI-MAIO, and this website, MAGIC OF ALKALINE, to Josh.

Advertise With Traffic Authority

Drive Unlimited Traffic to Your Real Business Website & Maximize Your Sales!

Are you ready to take your Business to the next level?

The secret to consistent sales and high-ticket commissions is quality traffic—and Traffic Authority delivers exactly that!

Why Traffic Authority?

100% Done-for-You Traffic – No need to chase leads!

Laser-Targeted Visitors – Attract buyers who are ready to take action.

Automated Traffic Flow – Set it up once and watch the leads roll in.

More Conversions - More Sales – Supercharge your Marketing results.

https://r1.trafficauthority.net/shinaicombat

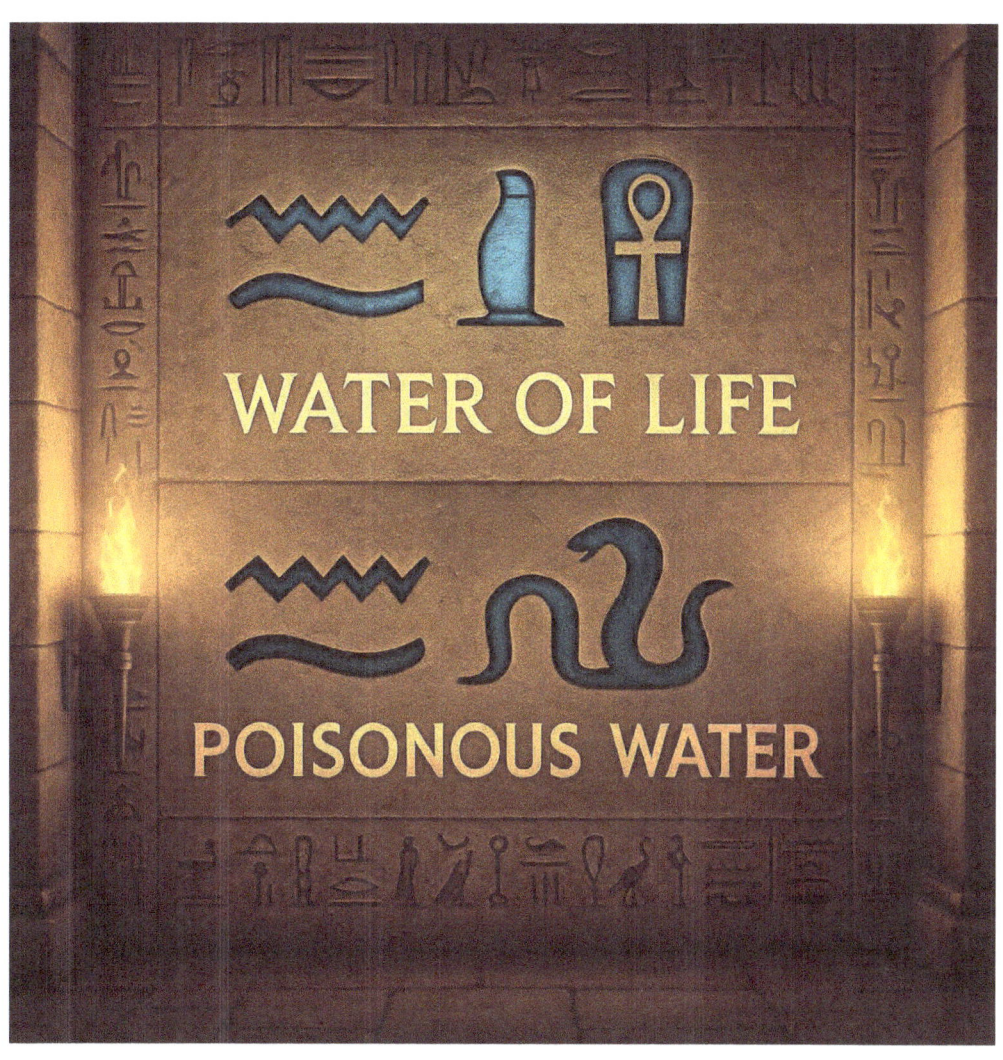

The Unseen Laws of Wealth

Sacred Rules the Elite Understand—But Never Speak Of.

☐ ☐ ☐ ☐

At first glance, it looks like just another online business…

But what if I told you this is the vehicle chosen by those who understand the real laws behind success, wealth, and impact?

Welcome to the Real Business Network —

Where ancient spiritual principles meet cutting-edge high-ticket profits.

The Law of Sacred Exchange

Don't expect massive abundance without first giving value.

This business delivers real, life-changing products—not empty promises or digital fluff.

What you give… returns tenfold.

The Law of Access

Not everyone should be invited into this unique sacred business.

That's why we offer an invitation-only model—so you work with people who respect the mission, are serious, and match your vibration.

The Law of Resonance

You attract what you embody.

If you're ready for high-ticket income, financial freedom, and spiritual alignment… this is calling you for a reason.

The Law of Timing

Opportunities like this don't wait forever.

The right time is the moment you recognize it.

Delay is spiritual debt.

The Law of Hidden Eyes

Even if no one sees your struggle, God, aka the universe, does.

And now, it's answering with a solution that pays you for changing lives.—

Watch the demo.

See the proof.

Feel the resonance.

This isn't just business—it's a spiritual transaction with real-world rewards.

155

Can You Truly Manifest Financial Abundance?

Beneath the stars… before the pyramids…

Humanity asked one question:

Can thought shape reality?

You've heard the words tossed around:

"Manifestation."

"Vibration."

"Abundance."

But what if it's not just hype?

What if these ancient structures — aligned with cosmic precision — were designed by those who understood the energetic blueprint of creation?

What if what we now call "The Law of Attraction" is simply a modern name for an ancient, divine formula buried in our DNA — and in the very stones of Giza?—

The Hidden Laws Behind Manifestation:

The Law of Attraction teaches that what you focus on expands.

But let's go deeper.

Because manifestation isn't just about thinking positively.

It's about aligning with universal laws that govern energy, matter, and money.

The Law of Vibration.

Everything is frequency.

Money is energy.

Health is energy.

Love is energy.

And the moment your frequency aligns with what you desire, it begins to magnetize toward you.

The Law of Reciprocity:

Give without expectation — and the universe returns it multiplied.

Value, generosity, service — these are not moral guidelines.

They're energy exchanges that trigger wealth in return.

The Law of Magnetic Action:

Your subconscious is a magnet.

You don't "chase" wealth — you attract it based on what you believe you are worthy of.

And most people are unconsciously magnetizing lack.

The Law of Clarity:

The more specific and clear your intention, the faster it becomes form.

Clarity turns chaos into creation.

Ambiguity delays abundance:

The universe delivers only what you're brave enough to ask for.

The Law of Inspired Action

Manifestation is not sitting still waiting.

It's moving with purpose. Acting with belief.

The moment you step forward in faith, doors swing open.—

Here's the secret no one's telling you:

Most people talk about the Law of Attraction… but never show you how to activate it.

We go beyond the theory.

We've fused ancient wisdom, biblical truth, real health breakthroughs, and a high-ticket business model into one unified system that empowers you with:

Financial Freedom — through a purpose-driven, high-commission structure.

Vibrational Health — with water technologies that activate your body at the cellular level.

Spiritual Alignment — reconnecting to the truths hidden in ancient Egypt, sacred scripture, and your own biology.

Imagine charging your body with the same life force Moses carried from Egypt…

Imagine generating income not from selling, but from aligning with a cause rooted in truth.

This is more than a brand.

More than a product.

More than a business.

It's a movement.

A vibration.

A frequency you were born to remember.

This Is Your Moment:

The Law of Attraction is already working — the question is:

Are you directing it… or drifting with it?

If you've been waiting for a sign, this is it.

Health - Wealth - Purpose - Alignment.

It doesn't start tomorrow.

It starts the moment you decide.

Daniel Di-Maio

daniel@magicofalkaline.com